I0687066

Smoke Signals

A John Tall Wolf Novel

Joseph Flynn

Stray Dog Press, Inc.
Springfield, IL
2019

PRAISE FOR JOSEPH FLYNN AND HIS NOVELS

"Flynn is an excellent storyteller." — *Booklist*

"Flynn propels his plot with potent but flexible force."
— *Publishers Weekly*

Digger
"A mystery cloaked as cleverly as (and perhaps better than)
any John Grisham work." — *Denver Post*

"Surefooted, suspenseful and in its breathless final moments
unexpectedly heartbreaking." — *Booklist*

The Next President
"*The Next President* bears favorable comparison to such
classics as *The Best Man, Advise and Consent* and
The Manchurian Candidate."
— *Booklist*

"A thriller fast enough to read in one sitting."
— *Rocky Mountain News*

The President's Henchman (A Jim McGill Novel)
"Marvelously entertaining." — *ForeWord Magazine*

JOSEPH FLYNN

SERIES

The Jim McGill Series
The President's Henchman, A Jim McGill Novel [#1]
The Hangman's Companion, A JimMcGill Novel [#2]
The K Street Killer A JimMcGill Novel [#3]
Part 1: The Last Ballot Cast, A JimMcGill Novel [#4 Part 1]
Part 2: The Last Ballot Cast, A JimMcGill Novel [#5 Part 2]
The Devil on the Doorstep, A Jim McGill Novel [#6]
The Good Guy with a Gun, A Jim McGill Novel [#7]
The Echo of the Whip, A Jim McGill Novel [#8]
The Daddy's Girl Decoy, A Jim McGill Novel [#9]
The Last Chopper Out, A Jim McGill Novel [#10]
The King of Mirth, A Jim McGill Novel [#11]

McGill's Short Cases 1-3

The Ron Ketchum Mystery Series
Nailed, A Ron Ketchum Mystery [#1]
Defiled, A Ron Ketchum Mystery Featuring John Tall Wolf [#2]
Impaled, A Ron Ketchum Mystery [#3]

The John Tall Wolf Series
Tall Man in Ray-Bans, A John Tall Wolf Novel [#1]
War Party, A John Tall Wolf Novel [#2]
Super Chief, A John Tall Wolf Novel [#3]
Smoke Signals, A John Tall Wolf Novel [#4]
Big Medicine, A John Tall Wolf Novel [#5]
Powwow in Paris, A John Tall Wolf Novel [#6]

The Zeke Edison Series
Kill Me Twice, A Zeke Edison Novel [#1]

STAND ALONE NOVELS

The Concrete Inquisition
Digger
The Next President
Hot Type
Farewell Performance
Gasoline, Texas
Round Robin, A Love Story of Epic Proportions
One False Step
Blood Street Punx
Still Coming
Still Coming Expanded Edition
Hangman — A Western Novella
Pointy Teeth, Twelve Bite-Size Stories

Dedication

In memory of Dad.

Acknowledgements

Catherine, Cat, Anne and Susan do their level best to catch all my typos and other mistakes, but I usually outwit them. Please be kind. Even Ty Cobb didn't get a hit every time at bat.

Author's Notes

This is a work of fiction. Neither the characters nor the Native American reservations named in the story are real. The Bureau of Indian Affairs, of course, exists within the United States Department of the Interior, and within the BIA its Office of Justice Services is "responsible for the overall management of the Bureau's law enforcement program," but my research turned up no one who has the job description I gave to John Tall Wolf. This mixture of fact and fiction falls under the heading of literary license. If you're a purist who demands complete realism, I recommend you stick to nonfiction, and good luck finding an author in that field who doesn't make mistakes or omissions.

As to a white male writing about Native American characters, that involves a bit of license, too. From my point of view, that license is rooted in our common humanity. If writers were to focus only on characters who shared their own backgrounds, we would establish a regime of literary apartheid.

AL
**Reader
Discretion
Advised**
Contains Adult
Language

Stray Dog Press, Inc.

Smoke Signals
A John Tall Wolf Novel
Published by Stray Dog Press, Inc., 2019
Springfield, IL 62704, U.S.A.

Copyright © kandrom, inc./Stray Dog Press, Inc.. 2013
All rights reserved

Author website: *www.josephflynn.com*

Flynn, Joseph
    Smoke Signals / Joseph Flynn
    226 pg.
    ISBN   978-0-9974500-8-8
    eBook 978-0-9908412-6-5

Printed in the United States of America

Without limiting the rights under copyright reserved above, no part of this publication may be reproduced, stored in or introduced into a retrieval system, or transmitted, in any form, or by any means (electronic, mechanical, photocopying, recording, or otherwise), without the prior written permission of both the copyright owner and the above publisher of this book.

PUBLISHER'S NOTE
This is a work of fiction. Names, characters, places, and incidents are either the product of the author's imagination or are used fictitiously; any resemblance to actual persons, living or dead, events, or locales is entirely coincidental.

Book design by Aha! Designs
Cover photo courtesy of www.istockphoto.com

Smoke Signals

A John Tall Wolf Novel

— CHAPTER 1 —

Friday, October 16, 2015
The Cascade Range — Washington State

By the time Bruno "Beebs" Bandi heard the crack of the rifle shot, the bullet had already zipped past his head, close enough for him to feel its passage. To Beebs' credit, he reacted in exactly the right way. He dived face first to the forest floor, instinctively throwing his hands out to keep his head and the camera dangling at his chest from harm. A second shot rang out. Beebs didn't feel this one whip by, but he had the distinct feeling there would have been a large hole in some vital part of him had he remained on his feet.

He rolled to his right, one hand shielding his camera, the other protecting his face. A third shot chased him into the Christmas tree shadow of a Douglas fir. The projectile scattered pine needles, humus and dirt inches from Beebs' backside. A fourth shot chewed off a chunk of bark sending splinters into the back of his left hand. He gritted his teeth to repress any cry of distress that might give away his position.

He didn't know who was shooting at him or why the SOB was doing it. All Beebs had been doing was walking in the freaking woods, taking pictures for the guy who owned the land. That dude, a young Silicon Valley tech billionaire, wanted Beebs to bring him some pictures of scenic spots which he might develop into sites for new communities of affordable housing. Cripes, who could get a hard-on about that?

Not that going off-road anywhere in the U.S. wasn't dangerous. Beebs had done his homework before he took the gig, which to be fair was paying him ridiculous money for what amounted to nothing more than assembling a landscape portfolio. Not that his pictures wouldn't be great, because they would. Beebs was a highly talented photographer.

He was somewhat notorious, too. Financial hardship had briefly nudged him into the sordid world of the paparazzi. He'd once climbed a tree in the resort town of Goldstrike, California to snap photos of a pair of young movie stars in the most intimate of moments. Those images, along with the camera he'd used, had been confiscated by the cops and never made public. Even so, word of what he'd done had gotten out and *imagining* what the coupling had looked like became an Internet game of global popularity.

The faces of the young actors were Photoshopped onto the bodies of innumerable porn performers. Beebs had been horrified and ashamed. He wished there might be some way he could make amends. He'd started his long slog to redemption by vowing never again to photograph anybody or anything except in the most flattering of lights.

That despite being offered a small fortune to work for Giles Henry, crown prince of tabloid reporters. For a moment, Beebs had been tempted, but then he'd learned Henry had been the prick who'd spread the word about Beebs going up that tree.

In spite of Beebs' decision to leave the dark side of the photographic arts, someone was now doing his damnedest to kill him. Christ, was it one of the young stars he'd humiliated? Or maybe it was *both* of them. The Internet game had pretty much run its course, but waiting for time to pass might have been the smart thing to do. The defamed parties would put distance between themselves and Beebs' murder that way.

The shooter, though, was getting closer. Beebs heard crunching leaves and snapping twigs, clear indications that footsteps were drawing near. The fact that the guy with the rifle wasn't even trying

to be stealthy said that he'd seen Beebs was unarmed. Probably had a scope on his weapon. He'd lined Beebs up in his crosshairs and ...
Missed?

What a goober. Beebs had never pulled the trigger of any firearm in his life, but he was sure if he'd had someone dead to rights he could have made the kill. So this dude must be really unskilled. That might have been enough to give Beebs a moment of hope. Only it wouldn't require *any* expertise to press the barrel of a rifle against someone's noggin and blow a hole in it.

On the other hand, if Beebs fought back that might put the sucker really off his game. While Beebs didn't carry a gun, he hadn't gone into the woods without any protection. There were wolves, bears and mountain lions in the Cascades; his research had told him that much. Not wanting to become a photographer tartare entrée to the fang and claw set, he'd taken precautions.

Beebs' cousin, Noah, owned a shop that sold novelty items, including stink bombs. For special customers who wanted to get even with people who deserved a special measure of vengeance, Noah concocted what he called *nuclear* stink bombs. There was no mushroom cloud, but Noah boosted the active ingredient, ammonium sulfide, and added several other noxious irritants.

"These things will stop a wild animal?" Beebs had asked his cousin.

Noah chuckled. "Knock King Kong right on his ass. You hold your nose, break the seal, throw it and run the hell away as fast as you can."

Praying his cousin had things right, Beebs added a grace note of his own to that plan. He got quietly to his feet. When he heard the guy who'd shot at him get maybe ten feet away, he gave his best impression of a blood-curdling scream. It was effective enough to get an immediate shot in reply. The bullet whistled past the tree providing Beebs' shelter. Immediately thereafter, Beebs leaped out from his hiding place. Startled by Beebs' sudden appearance, a stocky, round-faced Hispanic-looking guy holding a rifle without a scope took an involuntary step backward, tripped over some forest debris, landed on his back and lost hold of his weapon on impact.

The rifle came to rest equidistant between the two men, but Beebs didn't want to get into a wrestling match for it. The other guy might be stronger or have a knife. Beebs did exactly what Noah had told him to do. He threw the nuclear stink bomb at the shooter and ran the other way as fast as he could.

As he beat feet, Beebs heard the guy screaming.

— CHAPTER 2 —

Monday, October 19, 2015, Washington, DC

The Honorable Marlene Flower Moon, Acting Secretary of the Interior, smiled when John Tall Wolf entered her new office. John gave the furnishings a perfunctory once over. Lots of polished wood and high grade leather reflected the room's flattering lighting. A nine-foot long Lakota Sioux hunting lance tipped with a metal spearhead and fletched with eagle feathers was mounted on the wall behind Marlene's desk.

The Sioux and other Great Plains tribes used such lances to hunt buffalo, which by no coincidence, was the emblematic animal of the Department of the Interior. Marlene's symbolism couldn't have been more clear. In a bureaucracy employing 70,000 people, including the Bureau of Indian Affairs (BIA) and John Tall Wolf himself, she was the great chief who decided who lived and who died.

Professionally, of course.

Then another iconic item caught John's eye. On a bookshelf was a striking photo in a silver frame: the silhouette of a coyote in profile howling at a rising full moon. As an infant, John had been rescued by his adoptive parents from a coyote that had been about to have him for breakfast.

"Nice digs," John told Marlene, taking a guest chair without having been asked to sit. He glanced out a bank of windows at the Foggy Bottom landscape aglow in fall colors. "Terrific view."

Marlene beamed, revealing her oversized incisors. She'd considered her old office to have a lesser view than the one John's office had, once he'd been promoted to co-director of the BIA's Office of Justice Services, making him her bureaucratic equal. For a short time, anyway. Now, as her new office clearly showed, her official position was far superior to his.

Not that he gave a damn about such scaling of bureaucratic heights.

Taking a seat without her leave made that clear. Then again, Marlene would never be where she was without his intercession. John Tall Wolf was the White House's golden boy of the moment. Marlene took her seat and asked him, "How'd you do it, Tall Wolf, get the president to nominate me?"

"She asked who I thought would be good for the job."

"The president, not the vice president, asked you?"

"Right. I gave her your name, and Vice President Morrissey seconded my choice."

Marlene paused to consider that. Not just how much power-by-association Tall Wolf had acquired but how she might make the best use of his connection to the Oval Office.

"You don't have to say thank you," John told Marlene.

She didn't, instead asking, "Do you think the vice president will win the election next year?"

Become the next president, she meant.

John took a moment to give the question serious consideration.

"Always hard to answer that one. I think the other side will try to out-tough her with a macho candidate, but I don't think that will work. So, as a betting proposition, I'd have to give Jean Morrissey the edge, but not a big one."

"She's going to run on the Cool Blue ticket."

John hadn't heard that, wondered how Marlene had found out.

But then Marlene was Coyote, who always had her ways.

"If that's the case," he said, "I'd bump her edge up just a bit."

"But Cool Blue would limit her to one term."

"Didn't know that either." He thought Marlene should really serve the country as the Director of National Intelligence. The U.S. would be a much safer place if that happened. Focusing on the moment, though, he asked. "Are you already thinking of succeeding Jean Morrissey in the White House."

"It pays to plan ahead," Marlene said, "but I don't know if the country would elect *three* women in a row as president."

"Why not? The voters elected *forty*-three men in a row. And women are a majority of the electorate. They might think it's time to even things out."

Marlene smiled again, liking Tall Wolf's reasoning.

But she said, "You're cautioning me against trying to sabotage the vice president's campaign."

"That would be a terrible idea. Politically and personally."

Coyote was wily enough to understand both halves of John's message.

"Politically," she said, "because if Jean Morrissey loses, there will have been only one female president and that could be made to look like a regrettable fluke."

"Right."

"Personally, because I'd be fighting the vice president and you."

John didn't reply directly, only got to his feet and said, "If you asked me to stop by and see your new office as a social occasion, let me say again, it's terrific."

Marlene said, "Glad you like it, but sit back down. I have a job for you."

— CHAPTER 3 —

Calgary, Alberta — Canada

Royal Canadian Mounted Police Lieutenant Rebecca Bramley thought she had two things going for her at the informal disciplinary hearing in the deputy commissioner's office. One, the DC was a woman, Eileen Murphy. Two, Murphy, the highest ranking mountie in the province, had once been a victim of sexual harassment. One time that was publicly acknowledged anyway. More than a few members of the force, including Rebecca, had heard whispers that DC Murphy had toughed her way through any number of indignities in teeth-grinding silence.

Seated at the far end of the table from Rebecca was Sergeant Serge Marchand, the other principal player in the hearing. Between them were two brawny RCMP captains and a lawyer for each antagonist. Deputy Commissioner Murphy thought establishing the buffer zone was a wise move. As a result of underestimating Rebecca or overestimating himself, Marchand was already being referred to behind his back as "One-Nut."

Though not a part of the official record, that tidbit had made its way to the DC.

Costing a member of the force one of his testicles had not been well received by many of the mounties who still had two of them. There were some who felt otherwise, and Rebecca found that heartening. She hadn't mentioned her troubles to her fiancé, John Tall Wolf, but she was sure he would support her in the matter.

The deputy commissioner began by addressing the lawyers. "Have the two parties come to an informal resolution?" she asked.

Both lawyers shook their heads.

Marchand's advocate, Winton Royce, said, "That woman won't even apologize for the grievous, permanent injury she caused my client."

The deputy commissioner frowned at Royce and instructed him, "You will refer to Lieutenant Bramley by her proper title and name, sir, not as 'that woman'"

The lawyer nodded grudgingly.

Rebecca's attorney, Nellie Patrick, said, "Deputy Commissioner, the sergeant physically assaulted a superior officer. If anyone should apologize, it's him."

DC Murphy repressed a sigh. The matter was not going to get done the easy way.

"Very well. I've read both parties' official statements." Her eyes said she was sure they were written by the lawyers. "Now, I'll hear them describe the pertinent details aloud, in their own words." Seeing which one looks like more of a liar, she thought. "You go first, Sergeant Marchand."

The sergeant leaned forward to say his piece but remained seated.

Murphy said, "Please rise, Sergeant. Speak from your feet."

It was easier to observe body language that way, the DC knew. So did Marchand and he looked uneasy as he stood.

Rebecca kept her eyes on the deputy commissioner. She would read her de facto judge's face. That was more important than staring at Marchand. Nellie would watch him. They could compare notes after the hearing.

Marchand began, "I stopped into Tommy's Tip Top Tap, it was …" He paused. "Just under a month ago. Still can't believe what happened to me since then."

Winton Royce let his client indulge in self-commiseration but only for a moment.

He cleared his throat and Marchand continued. "I stopped in for a pop. A drink. My usual after a day on the job."

"Was that establishment the first place you stopped in for a *pop*, Sergeant?" the DC asked.

Marchand clear his throat and said, "No, ma'am. I stopped at Fast Eddie's before that."

"Just one drink at each place?"

"Yes, ma'am."

"What kind of drinks?"

"Dewars at Eddie's; Labatt Blue at Tommy's."

"So a shot and a beer."

"Yes, ma'am."

Royce added, "Separated by twenty minutes driving time, Deputy Commissioner."

DC Murphy gave the lawyer a mirthless smile. "I noticed that in the written statement."

Telling him to keep quiet without saying so.

"You're at Tommy's having a beer, Sergeant. Please continue."

"I was at the bar talking with a couple of friends and I saw ..." Marchand lapsed into silence again. His face sagged in regret. Collecting himself, he continued, "I saw Constable Grace Dorland. I'd reprimanded her harshly earlier that week. I thought I should go over and apologize to her."

"The criticism concerned the performance of Constable Dorland's official duties?" the DC asked.

"Yes, ma'am. Constable Dorland pulled over a driver for speeding. Turned out he was a wanted criminal, had a record as an arsonist. He's suspected of setting the —"

"Fire at our favorite junior Western Hockey League team's rink," the DC said. "The suspicion was an unscrupulous rival had paid for the blaze. It's something of a national scandal, isn't it?"

Marchand decided it was time to inspect the shine on his shoes. "Yes, ma'am."

"What was the nature of your rebuke to Constable Dorland, Sergeant?"

He looked up and said, "She approached the speeder's car alone; she should have had her partner, the senior man in the car, Corporal McKee, with her. She might have been hurt handling things the way she did. I went off on her when I heard the details, harder than I should have. I went over to her at Tommy's to say I was sorry, but also to tell her she had to be more careful in the future."

Marchand was about to continue his story, but DC Murphy held up a hand.

"Please be seated, Sergeant. We'll let Lieutenant Bramley pick up the narrative from here."

Rebecca got to her feet. "I was sitting with my back to the sergeant, but I saw him coming."

"How did you manage that, Lieutenant?"

"I was watching him in a mirror, a Moosehead Beer mirror."

Winton Royce raised his hand, wanting to be heard.

"Yes, Mr. Royce?"

"Deputy Commissioner, I checked that mirror under the same lighting conditions that existed on the night in question. I could barely see my secretary, whom I positioned at the bar where Sergeant Marchand was standing."

DC Murphy turned to Rebecca. "Lieutenant?"

"I have 20-10 vision, ma'am. Perhaps Mr. Royce doesn't see quite so well. I saw Sergeant Marchand quite clearly. We could do a comparative test of visual acuity, Mr. Royce's and mine, right now, if you like."

"Mr. Royce?" the deputy commissioner asked.

The lawyer declined the opportunity, losing the point he'd tried to make.

"Proceed with your account, Lieutenant," the DC said.

"Sergeant Marchand approached our table and stood approximately one foot behind me. Constable Dorland was on the far side of the table. Sergeant Marchand began to address Constable Dorland in a crude and provocative manner."

"In what way crude, Lieutenant?"

"He said, 'Puck bunny, you're in more trouble than you know. You better change your story fast or you'll be well and truly fucked.'"

Puck bunny was a common variation on the slur puck slut. A hockey player groupie who put out for the guys.

District Commissioner Murphy, from the grim expression on her face, was all too familiar with the term, but she asked Rebecca, "How did you know the comment wasn't directed at you, Lieutenant?"

"I had no story to change, ma'am, and the sergeant told me to get lost or I'd find out whose family was really wired into the powers that be on the force."

The DC directed a brief, evil look at Marchand before turning back to Rebecca.

"You weren't intimidated by this threat, Lieutenant?"

Rebecca smiled. "In the best Monty Python fashion, ma'am, I farted in his general direction."

The deputy commissioner rocked with silent laughter, as if she'd staged the whole informal inquiry just to hear that comment. Nonetheless, she continued: "And how did Sergeant Marchand react to that?"

"He took it in shocked silence for a moment, but when my niece, Constable Dorland, started to laugh at him, he clapped an open hand on my right shoulder. Hard enough to leave a bruise. That was when he told me, 'Get out of here now, Bramley, or I'm going to bend you over that table and ram all my nine inches right up your ass.'"

Royce thought about objecting, but the look on the deputy commissioner's face told him he'd only be making a bad situation worse. He held his tongue. So did Marchand.

"How did you respond, Lieutenant?"

"I got out of my chair, shoved it aside and bent over the table ... because that made it easier to execute a mule-kick into the sergeant's crotch. Caught him a good one, too, from what I hear."

Royce and both of the captains had to get to their feet when Marchand popped out of his chair. It took the sergeant only a second to realize he'd made a mistake, but by then it was too late. He'd shown himself to be a hothead.

Deputy Commissioner Murphy pointed him back to his seat and he took it.

"Do you have anything else to say, Lieutenant Bramley?" she asked.

"I know you're trying to get to the truth here, ma'am, so I have a suggestion."

"What's that?"

"If the two captains providing security here today don't object, why don't you ask them to see if Sergeant Marchand really has nine inches to his name? If he's lying about that, how can you take his word about anything else?"

In a hallway after the hearing, with Marchand having been escorted outside and his altered manhood still officially unexamined, Nellie Patrick told her client, "You did very well in there today, Rebecca, kept your cool and got that big idiot to lose his, but he does have his family behind him. There are dozens of them on the force and more than a few are highly placed and have a lot of pull."

Rebecca said, "That's what got all this started in the first place. That hoser Marchand is related to a lot of achievers while he's been stuck in grade for years. He wanted to claim the credit for apprehending that firebug Grace nabbed. When she wouldn't fudge her report the way he wanted, he got nasty."

Nellie pointed out, "He did get McKee to back his version."

"McKee's lying. The truth will come out soon enough. McKee's not tough enough to keep up a false front. Meanwhile, I'll enjoy my paid involuntary leave."

"Rebecca, I would be lying if I said I wasn't concerned how this might turn out."

"Okay, Nellie, you be concerned," Rebecca said. "I'm not going to worry about it."

"Really? You've got something to fall back on if you lose your job?"

"Yeah, if worse comes to worse, I'll flee south, get married and become an American."

— CHAPTER 4 —

The Cascade Range — Washington State

We should shoot the poor *cabrón* and burn his body," Basilio Nuñez said.

He was the second in command and tended to be impulsive.

Julián Fortuna, his more thoughtful cousin and the operation's boss, said, "Really? Perhaps you haven't noticed we are having a dry autumn, after several years of drought. If we didn't have the water we divert from the few remaining streams, we would already be out of business, and you want to start a fire. Set the whole valley and the nearby mountains ablaze, perhaps."

Julián's tone had been mild, but Basilio knew he'd been scolded nonetheless.

"We cook every day," he replied. "Sometimes with an open flame." He wrinkled his nose. "As it is, I won't be able to eat anything until we get rid of that stench."

Both men gazed in the direction of the miserable Ernesto Batista who sat on the ground, leaning against the trunk of a tree and pulling his knees up to his chest, as if he was trying to squeeze the vile odor out of himself. As yet, he had not succeeded. Unable to get away from his own stink, he looked as if he might succumb to it. Then he'd have to be buried. That would improve the air quality but it would be bad for camp morale.

Julián and Basilio were responsible to their bosses in Mexico. For a second year, they'd had 10,000 cannabis plants under cultivation, planted in the spring, brought along from seedlings to flowering plants and harvested just when the THC was at its height. It was a painstaking process. That's why all the illegal immigrants they used had been farmers back in Mexico.

The peasants knew how to get the most out of the ground they tilled. If they performed well for a year, their coyote debts would be repaid and they would be free to go. Or, if they chose, they could stay and receive a salary in cash, far more than they ever could have made back home or working in *El Norte* as landscapers or manual laborers for the gringos. If they had ambition and showed the aptitude, they could become guards, as Batista had done.

The armed men received twice the salary the farmers did. They kept intruders out and the work force onsite and orderly. What everyone who worked under the two *jefes* had in common was living under the threat of horrific vengeance against them and their families if they ever told the police — or anyone else — about the marijuana growing operation.

The original site for the illegal cultivation that Julián and Emilio had run was in a national park in California, but local environmentalists had stumbled upon them, escaped and made it impossible for the state and federal governments to ignore what was going on there. Stinking tree-huggers. Julián, Basilio and their indentured workers had to flee. The cousins had to look for opportunities in other remote places.

Julián, a thinker, was the one who'd had the notion of taking the operation onto a private land holding. Why not go where some fat, rich gringo had more land than he ever got around to looking at? Julián had fleetingly considered suggesting to the bosses that they *buy* the land and conceal the true ownership by using shell companies as fronts. But where was the fun in that?

Yes, making money was the objective, but for any real criminal what made getting out of bed in the morning a pleasure was taking advantage of the fools who played by the rules. A genuine crook's goals were twofold: have things your own way and laugh all the way to the bank. Using numbered accounts, of course.

Julián had understood the implications of the new law in Washington state that had legalized marijuana. Profits back home were going to take a big hit. He was right about that. In the first year after the law went into effect, marijuana revenues were down 20%, and things would only get worse. The new market environment demanded new ways to compete.

He came to three conclusions as to how best to do that: Use illegals to keep labor costs to a minimum; lower transportation expenses by growing locally; and eliminate the overhead of buying real estate by expropriating it from the true owner without him ever becoming aware. Enforce your claim at the point of a gun if the *pendejo* caught on. These would become the rules of the game.

Rules were perfectly fine if you were the one making them up.

There was one more strategy Julián recognized as a necessity. You had to build your brand. Having a colloquial command of American English, he named his product *Holy Smokes,* and designed a logo of Jesus toking up, the smoke from the joint in his hand forming a halo above his head. Believers and atheists alike seemed to like the joke. Sales were brisk.

Perhaps Julián would be damned to hell for such sacrilege, if there really was a time of judgment upon leaving this life, but at the moment he was still young and unconcerned about such an outcome. He focused on returning to Mexico three years hence as a very rich man.

Dreaming of success was the most addictive drug of all.

Julián said, "Batista is the one with the wife: *muy guapa,* no?"

Very pretty.

Basilio nodded. "*Sí.* How one such as her could share herself with one such as him …"

He had to shake his head at the injustice. Basilio would have loved to … but he couldn't. His cousin would have set *him* on fire if he ever tried. Julián had explained things to him. The people who worked for them were indentured for their first year of labor.

Thereafter, they were held in thrall by the threat that they would be killed horribly if they talked to the police.

That burdensome necessity being the case, it was best for business to make the workers' circumstances as agreeable as possible. See that they were adequately fed, that their medical needs were tended. Short of any betrayal on their part, never threaten their welfare or the sanctity of their marriages and families. Give them a better life than they'd ever known. Bind them to you with affection as well as fear. Two motivations always worked better than one.

Julián had graduated from the best business school on the West Coast.

Basilio was just smart enough to follow his cousin's lead.

Julián said, "Ask *Señora* Batista to fetch her husband, take him to a stream and bathe him. Make it one of the more distant rivulets. We don't want our agricultural water to be polluted. Ask the señora to please help scrub her husband as best she can."

Julián saw the look in his cousin's eyes. He was imagining the woman's hands all over him.

"Basilio, you will not say an improper word to Batista's wife, not one. Nor will you ever come close to touching her."

Being caught out, Basilio could only feign indignation and say, "Of course, not, Julián. I know the rules."

"Never forget them, not for a moment. We are doing quite well. You will become rich along with me."

"*Sí*." Basilio knew his cousin was right. He might not become as wealthy as Julián, but there was no question he would have more money than he could ever spend. There were other women even prettier than Batista's wife. He would be able to afford any number of them.

Even so, as he went to fetch Valeria, he had a depressing thought.

None of those other women would be available tonight or anytime soon.

Still, Basilio was also doubly motivated: affection and fear.

He would be nothing but polite and hands-off to Señora Batista.

For his part, Julián was thinking about the men he'd sent out to capture the intruder.

He'd have felt better if the prick had been carrying a gun instead of a camera.

— CHAPTER 5 —

Department of the Interior — Washington, DC

What's the job? John Tall Wolf asked.

Marlene Flower Moon had her own question. "Have you ever heard of Frederic Strait?"

John shook his head. "Never."

"He's a brilliant young man, only twenty-five and already a multi-billionaire."

"You have a knack for making rich friends," John said. "A useful talent for someone with political ambitions."

John encouraged Marlene's presidential dreams. Toiling in the Oval Office would leave her little time to think about him. Even Coyote would be stressed hewing to a president's work schedule. Still, she'd have fun matching her wiles against those of other world leaders.

"I'm building a war chest," Marlene admitted.

"So Mr. Strait has a problem you want me to solve and he'll be grateful to you if I do. How's that supposed to fall under the scope of my duties with the Bureau of Indian Affairs?"

"Mr. Strait has a few things in common with you."

Getting an uneasy feeling, John asked, "Such as?"

"He and his mother are Cheyenne. She was adopted as a pregnant fourteen-year-old by a white couple. She'd been turned out by her parents for disgracing them."

John frowned. "Was the biological father white?"

Marlene shook her head. "But he wasn't Cheyenne either. The girl wouldn't say who he was."

John had come to have some idea of who his own paternal family was, but that had happened only by the time he'd reached his mid-thirties. He asked, "This guy wants me to find out who his dad is or was?"

"No, I'm going to do that," Marlene said.

John had no doubt Marlene would succeed. "So what is it you want me to do and, by the way, how'd this guy I've never heard of make all his money?"

Marlene smiled, flashing her predatory dentition. "He changed his name to get more in touch with his true heritage. Now, he calls himself Freddie Strait Arrow."

John smiled. "I like his sense of humor, but I still don't know him."

"To answer your other question, Freddie made his money in high tech. As a student at Rensselaer Polytechnic, he patented a microchip with what I'm told is a revolutionary architecture. Does all sorts of things better than other chips. Freddie says its just the first in a series of advances he has in mind. The licensing agreements he's reached with several big corporations made him wealthy."

"Good for the smart Indian kid," John said. "He have any plans for investing his fortune other than making you president? He does know what you have in mind, right?"

Marlene nodded. "He thinks it's a marvelous idea."

John was sure at that moment that Marlene had seduced Freddie.

"You might like his other big plan for the future," Marlene said.

John said, "So tell me. What's he got in mind?"

"He's not going to take the country back from the white man; he's going to *buy* it back."

John kept a straight face. "He'll need a powerful sum to do that. Billions would be just a drop in the bucket."

Marlene said, "He might forgo Kansas and North Dakota."

John grinned and played along. "He could start small, buy Rhode Island and Delaware, just to show his intent."

"Okay, nobody will ever be rich enough to buy the whole country," Marlene said.

"Glad we agree on that much," John replied.

"But he has been buying large holdings in New York City."

John laughed and slapped a knee. "Freddie's trying to buy back Manhattan? All right, you've got me. I at least want to meet him."

"He's buying land all around the country," Marlene continued. "The idea is by the time he's an old man and maybe the richest person in the world, he'll deed all his purchases back to the tribes that originally held the land. That way, they'll form an archipelago of sovereign Native American nations right across the United States."

John whistled softly. "I can see where that might be tied up in court for a century or two, but I do admire the young man's pluck and vision. So how do I fit into this grand scheme?"

Marlene began, "Freddie owns two mountains and the valley between them in Washington State ..."

— CHAPTER 6 —

The Cascade Range — Washington State

Showing great spousal devotion and a strong stomach, Valeria Batista led her husband, Ernesto, by the hand to the stream where he was to be cleansed of the vile odor that enveloped him. Basilio Nuñez had the job of watching over them. Valeria had arrived in the mountains of *El Norte* a year after her husband had come to the United States. The price of being smuggled into California and then up the coast to Washington had doubled from what it had cost Ernesto a year earlier, and as beautiful as Valeria was a premium had to be paid to see that she arrived unmolested.

Trailing along behind the couple at safe distance, Basilio called out.

"*Señora,* do you by chance have any sisters?"

His thinking was perhaps her beauty might be shared by a sibling.

The Batistas stopped and turned to look at Basilio.

"Three," Valeria replied, knowing just what the *pendejo* — moron — had in mind. "I am the plain one of my family."

Basilio's jaw dropped at the idea, and then it firmed as he thought she had to be toying with him. Still, the notion had such allure he couldn't help but revisit it. If it was true, he wanted to see all three sisters. One would be enough to make his own, but if he had the opportunity to select his favorite, what could be better?

"Would they like to come to America?" he asked.

"What? Up here in this wilderness? I would not have come except to be with Ernesto."

There it was again, Basilio thought, the inexplicable attraction of a peasant for such a beauty. Batista might have been kind, even indulgent, to his wife, but was that enough? Of course, he might be hung like an Andalusian bull, but that, too, would be fate playing a joke.

"Perhaps they could be housed in Los Angeles or San Francisco," Basilio suggested. "I am quite rich, you know."

Valeria dared to offer a skeptical look, but she played another angle. "*Señor,* are you saying my sisters would live in a fine house, but their sister, me, and my husband, Ernesto, would be stuck up here in this cold forest with wild animals?"

Basilio saw that not only was Valeria beautiful, she could also drive a hard bargain. But that only encouraged him. A beautiful woman with spirit was even more desirable than one who was meek and submissive.

To show her his wealth and power, Basilio said, "I will pay off your coyote debt, and all of you will live together, even him." Meaning Ernesto.

Valeria gave Basilio a long, hard look. "You swear this, before God?"

He raised a hand. "I do, before God."

"I will test the truth of your words."

"How?" Basilio asked, suspicion entering his voice.

"When we get to the stream, I will need to bathe my husband. If you are a man of honor, someone my sisters should know, you will not watch us. You will stay somewhere you are unable to see us and you will wait until we are dressed again before taking us back to camp."

Making that concession would not be easy for Basilio. Seeing Valeria, splashing naked in a stream, would be a sight to behold. Certainly, it was one he had been looking forward to, and one he would never forget. Of course, Ernesto would also be nude, and that would be something he'd never want to see or remember.

"Very well, but one more thing." Basilio had to bargain to maintain some self-respect.

"What?"

"As long as you are cleaning yourselves, make sure you clean that weapon, too."

Ernesto still carried the semi-auto assault carbine he'd been issued. It also had been suffused with the noxious odor. Ernesto spoke for the first time, saying humbly, *"Sí, patrón."*

Basilio sat on a round rock in a small meadow and let a half-mile gap grow between himself and the Batistas.

Giving the husband and wife room to whisper.

"You can not ever go back to these people, you know that?" Valeria asked.

Ernesto nodded and said, "Neither can you."

"Why did you not shoot the man in the forest?"

"I tried to scare him off. He was little more than a boy, and he carried only a camera, not a gun." Ernesto shrugged. "Some men you shoot, others you don't."

"Had you known what he would do to you …"

"Yes, then, of course."

"So you did not miss because your aim was poor?"

Ernesto only gave his wife a look. She knew who he was. He'd been a farmer as a boy in Mexico, but as a man he'd been a Mexican marine. His identity had been exposed. A bounty was put on his head; self-imposed exile had become a necessity.

"You know why I love you, don't you?" she asked.

"Because I saved you from one such as the bastard behind us."

"And asked nothing in return. You did not miss your shot that day."

"Nor will I miss any other I need to make."

The Batistas disappeared from Basilio's view behind a growth of shrubs rising at the edge of the stream. Basilio gave them ninety minutes before he went looking for them. He figured that was time enough for a bath, a screw and a second bath. That was the limit of both his courtesy and his patience. The *señora* would simply have to understand.

By the time he got to the rivulet, though, she and her damn husband were long gone.

The peasant's rifle had vanished with them.

Julián was not going to like this.

— CHAPTER 7 —

Dulles International Airport — Washington, DC

John Tall Wolf was lucky enough to snag a ride on an executive jet. Marlene had arranged it; Freddie Strait Arrow had provided the aircraft, a Gulfstream G550. The seat in which John sat was fully reclinable and able to accommodate his six-foot-four-plus length. Once the plane reached cruising altitude on its way to Seattle-Tacoma International Airport, he'd lie back and take a nap.

Before the G550 could leave its gate, though, the petite and exquisite cabin attendant named Nan approached him and said, "Sir, the captain has a request to delay departure."

John had the feeling Marlene was not responsible for the delay.

She'd simply appear in a puff of smoke if she really wanted to see him.

"What's holding us up, Nan?"

The attendant had introduced herself as he'd boarded the aircraft.

"A woman, sir. She's just arrived at the airport herself, flying in from Calgary. She called your office and was told you were about to depart Washington. Her name is—"

"Rebecca Bramley."

"Yes, sir. She said she hoped to visit with you here in town, and she'd like to see you, if at all possible, before we depart. She was very polite."

"She has terrific manners, but she could also punch a grizzly bear in the nose."

"Oh, my. If I may say so, sir, the captain told me Ms. Bramley sounded a bit crestfallen when she heard you were about to leave town."

John frowned. Sadness was not a prominent feature of his fiancée's emotional repertoire. "At the risk of throwing people's schedules out of whack, yes, let's delay our departure. That's all right with the pilot, isn't it?"

"Of course, sir. This plane is yours to use as you see fit. That was Mr. Strait Arrow's explicit instruction."

Must be nice to be twenty-five and have a luxury aircraft to lend to people, John thought. But at the moment he was pleased the whiz kid was affording him some flexibility. He told Nan, "We might be having another passenger fly west with us. We have everything necessary to make her comfortable, I assume."

Nan smiled and said, "Absolutely, sir."

John took out his phone and Nan gave him space to speak privately.

Rebecca picked up and John told her, "I know you just got off a plane, but getting on the one I'm taking to Seattle will be anything but a hardship, and I certainly want to hear why you came all the way to Washington unannounced to see me. We're not breaking up, are we?"

"Never." Rebecca asked for directions to John's gate.

He said he'd come and escort her back to his magic carpet.

— CHAPTER 8 —

The Cascade Range — Washington State

Julián Fortuna, being the high honors graduate of the best business school on the West Coast that he was, had made plans to evacuate the *campesinos,* the processed marijuana, next year's seedlings, all the agricultural tools, residential tents, food, water and other necessities, along with the odd two or three million in cash on hand, should unforeseen circumstances arise. Three alternate sites of operation had been found. All of them fell under the ownership of the same private citizen as the original location.

The other settings ranged from nearby to far away, from less than easy to find to deeply hidden and hellish to attack. Thing was, Julián had never expected to need any of them. Making sure he had options was, he'd thought, a simple exercise in prudence.

The kind of thing that failing to do would surely bite you on the ass, but once provided for should be nothing more than a way to sleep easy. Now, the whole stinking process was well under way. The peasants had been warned not to run away, and Julián himself had spread the lie to the campesinos that Ernesto and Valeria had been shot when they had tried to escape.

He'd pointed out Basilio as the heartless executioner who had killed them.

"This man," he'd told the assembled clandestine community, "is a cold-blooded killer, as am I. Anyone who disobeys us will die, painfully."

Julián truly hated this approach to management. It absolutely destroyed team spirit. He would have to work like a sonofabitch to get an atmosphere of good feelings back. In the meantime, productivity would suffer and revenue would take a dive.

If their little company had been listed on a stock exchange, the shares would have tanked. Even without that stigma, the bosses in Mexico wouldn't like the decline in the cash-flow one bit. They would blame Julián when, really, it was his idiot cousin's fault.

"How the hell could you let them escape?" he'd asked Basilio when the numbskull had first slinked back into camp.

Hanging his head, Basilio said, "She made me promise I wouldn't look."

Julián was incredulous. "Valeria Batista? She was the one giving orders? I don't remember making her your superior."

Julián had spoken so quietly no one outside his tent could hear, but Basilio was sure everyone would hear the gunshot if his cousin killed him. Of course, Basilio was the one who'd actually killed people, several men and one woman, while Julián had never done more than give one *cabron* a few whacks with a baseball bat.

Part of that disparity, Basilio couldn't deny, was because Julián was smart enough to get his way without having to kill people.

"*Lo siento,*" Basilio said. I'm sorry.

Julián sighed and strained to understand the situation. "What did she promise you so you would not watch her bathe with her husband? My first impulse is to think sex, but I don't see her doing that in front of her man. Even Ernesto Batista would not stand for it."

Still staring at his feet, Basilio confessed. "She said she would arrange for her three sisters to come from Mexico and stay with me." He raised his head and conjured a small, gullible smile. "She said she is the plain one among them."

Julián sighed and tried to ease his worsening headache by rubbing his temples.

"Cousin, did you ever stop to think the woman might not have *any* sisters?"

Just the idea was enough to stupefy Basilio. He opened his mouth to speak but could not find the right words. When he finally did there was only one. *"¡Puta!"*

Whore!

Julián's thoughts ran along a more practical path. The fact that a woman who was supposed to be an illiterate farmer's wife had so deftly manipulated Basilio reflected badly on him as well as his cousin. In business, as in life, there were times when it was easy to feel that powers greater than yourself were screwing with you. Using you as an object of contemptuous amusement.

First there was the fellow in the forest with his camera. He seemingly appeared out of nowhere. A lack of nearby hiking paths was one of Julián's first considerations in choosing the site for his operation. Nonetheless, up popped a man with a camera. Who then got the better of an armed guard who had managed to take several shots at him.

Then the guard himself, and his wife, became the first workers to escape the encampment.

What next? It was all too easy to imagine things growing progressively worse. So there was no question that the operation would have to move, and not to the nearest alternative either. They would have to retreat to the most distant site. Just getting there would be hard on everyone. Working the land would be much more difficult, as would guarding the workforce. Productivity would drop even further, but there was no other choice.

Well, maybe there was one thing to do. Shoot Basilio if it looked like he'd be a continuing source of either horrible judgment or plain bad luck. Scapegoating might be an ancient practice, but it was still a tool of modern business.

They got the whole operation packed up and moving in less than 24 hours.

— CHAPTER 9 —

38,000 feet over Oregon

Two of the seats in the Gulfstream not only reclined, the arm rests between them folded up and tucked out of the way with the result being a double bed done in butter-soft leather. Nan, the flight attendant, brought out pillows and blankets, retreated to a nook near the cockpit and John and Rebecca took a snooze for the first two-thirds of the flight. No hanky-panky involved. That would have been uncouth. Still, Rebecca snuggled into John's embrace and stayed there.

The pilots provided a flight smooth enough not to disturb their slumber.

After waking, righting their seats and refreshing themselves, Rebecca told John her story.

He listened carefully and agreed with her surmise that as things stood she might be forced out of the RCMP or transferred to a duty post so disagreeable she'd resign. Then he asked, "You want me to fix things for you?"

She gave him a look and asked, "You've got connections on the force higher than Serge Marchand's?"

"Not directly. But you just had an election up in Canada, didn't you?"

"Yes, but I didn't think anyone down here noticed, even you."

"Probably wouldn't have, but the *Washington Post* ran the results in the sports section, next to the hockey scores."

Rebecca smiled, but still gave him a punch on the shoulder. A soft one, in case he had a trick as well as an arm up his sleeve.

"Okay, tell me what you're thinking," she said.

"I've been making friends in high places since I moved to Washington."

"How high?"

"The president."

Rebecca's gaze took on a searching quality, as if looking for a joke. Her next sock at the guy sitting next to her might be a hard one. "Are you kidding me?"

John shook his head. He told her of working with Jim McGill, not getting too specific about the details, but saying, "I met the president after we wrapped things up. I know the VP, too, and my money says she'll be the next president. I put in a good word for Marlene to become the Secretary of the Interior and she got the nomination."

"Yeah, I read that, but I didn't know you were behind it."

John had to smile. He did know about a new prime minister being elected in Canada, probably would have taken notice in any case, but had paid special attention because of his engagement to Rebecca. After all, there was some chance he might move up there when he and Rebecca got married.

What impressed him, though, was that she had noticed Marlene's nomination.

He couldn't say whether the PM of Canada even had a cabinet.

"I've got a Google alert on Marlene," Rebecca added.

John smiled. He'd told his sweetheart that Marlene had tried to seduce him more than once. Rebecca didn't care that much about American politics. She was keeping an eye out for her guy.

"Probably wise," John said. "I should do the same. Anyway, with my connections at the top of the U.S. government, and reading more than the sports section, I know relations between our countries are supposed to improve with the election of your new PM. I could ask President Grant or VP Morrissey for a little favor. Get things straightened out for you with the RCMP or maybe make you

Canada's new Secretary of the Interior."

"Minister of the Interior," Rebecca corrected him.

"I'll make a note of that."

"That's sweet of you, thinking of me in such grand terms, but I just want to be a cop, a good one. Honest, trustworthy and all that." John leaned back for a bit of perspective. "So you're going to let the chips fall where they may?"

She nodded. "That's the only way I'll see if I can get a fair shake."

John kissed his fiancée, sat back and leaned his shoulder against hers.

He said quietly, "If you don't get one, I'll travel north and scalp this Marchand creep. Leave him with one nut and no hair."

Rebecca laughed, kissed John's cheek and said, "I promise not to tell on you if you do, but can you share with me what you're up to right now? Or do I have to fly home spinning fantasies about your glamorous doings? I mean, jetting around in a plane like this and all."

"Let's get some drinks first, and then we can give Nan the rest of the flight off."

— CHAPTER 10 —

The Ritz-Carlton — Washington, D.C.

Freddie Strait Arrow and Marlene Flower Moon wore hotel bathrobes. Marlene had her wet hair wrapped in a towel. Freddie reclined against an arm of a sofa, his feet on Marlene's lap. She was rubbing them. To Freddie, that felt almost as good as what had transpired in the bedroom and the shower.

"You're sure you don't want to run in 2016?" Freddie asked.

At twenty-five, he looked like he still could pass for a teenager. He was tall and thin with a mop of black hair that might have been modeled after Paul McCartney's early Beatle days. His face still had traces of baby fat around the jawline, but his eyes shone with an intelligence so radiant that looking at them directly was almost as hard as staring at the sun.

For most people, anyway. Marlene held their gaze without difficulty.

"I'm sure. I can wait. Five years isn't a long time," she said.

Marlene didn't say she was unsure she could beat Jean Morrissey, especially with Tall Wolf working on the vice president's side. In five years, if Morrissey kept her promise to serve only one term, there would be no formidable female candidate to oppose her. Marlene had scouted the political landscape to make sure of that.

As for now, she was content to cultivate Freddie. She would make him stronger and more practiced in the ways of the world.

All in all, he would come to resemble Tall Wolf. Only without the adversarial edge. And with infinitely more money.

Money being the mother's milk of politics, as a wise man from California once said.

She told Freddie, "A couple of years experience at Interior and then a step up in the next president's cabinet, say State Department, will stand me in good stead for a run in 2020."

"So you're going to help Jean Morrissey?"

"Yes, and be a very good soldier."

Tall Wolf would see Marlene's underlying plan, both in her political choice and binding rich, young Freddie to her, but Tall Wolf wouldn't try to block either move. Sooner rather than later, he might even begin to relax, thinking he'd become less important to her. Perhaps even feeling she'd lost interest in him.

That would never happen, of course. But if she could lull Tall Wolf's suspicion of her so much the better. Her reverie vanished as a bright chiming sound disturbed the cozy silence.

"Text," Freddie told her.

He took a phone out of a pocket in his robe and looked at the screen.

"My photographer," he said. "The guy I sent out to scope the situation on my property." Freddie frowned and looked at Marlene. "Some prick shot at him. Five times."

Marlene stopped rubbing Freddie's feet. "How did he get away?"

Freddie's eyes scurried down the text and he laughed. "Beebs, that's the photog's name, hit the shooter with a stink bomb. Heard him howling as he ran away."

Marlene moved Freddie's legs to the floor, forcing him to sit up.

She told him, "So you were right. There are trespassers on your property."

"Gotta be pot farmers," Freddie said, "Climate's wrong for coca plants and poppies. Could be somebody cooking meth, but we didn't get the right heat signature for that."

Freddie had commissioned a satellite survey of his property, just as a point of general curiosity. He wanted to get a different look at the land he'd bought. A photo analyst from the satellite company had told him, "You've got an infestation."

She hadn't meant ash borers or any other insectile pest.

"People. If they aren't yours, chances are they're up to no good. A drug operation is the most likely situation; a cult of paranoid and-or homicidal loonies is possible but less likely. Either way, you ought to call the cops."

Freddie had decided to hold off on local law enforcement. He went to the woman who had approached him at a tech conference and told him she was going to run for president, saying she needed a billionaire to back her. She'd said she was going to give him the best sex he would ever have in his life. The offer of bliss, she said, came with no strings attached. If he wasn't happy with it, she'd go away and find someone else.

At first, Freddie thought Marlene was too old for him. Then, like she could read his mind and he'd stepped into a movie, she became younger right in front of his eyes. Pretty good trick, he'd thought, and he wanted to find out how she'd done it. Besides that, he was sure no sex could be so good that it would make him her lapdog.

He was pretty much wrong about that.

Being with Marlene was magical, sometimes in a truly scary way.

He still told himself he could leave her any time he wanted … only he hadn't and it had been six months now. His new rationale became that even the best sex in the world had to get old eventually, and then he'd reassert his independence. It was going to happen any day, week or month now. In the meantime, he'd enjoy what he had.

So he went to Marlene for help dealing with the trespassers.

She thought it would be an impressive story to tell at her confirmation hearing, how she'd aided in breaking up a drug gang. Start her new job with a bang. She put Tall Wolf on the case.

Oh, and the idea to buy land around the country and give it away to native tribes?

Marlene had given it to Freddie.

— CHAPTER 11 —

Inn at the Market, Seattle, — Washington State

That's pretty cool," Rebecca told John as they settled into their hotel room, "buying land and giving it back to the original owners. Maybe some rich guy in Canada could do the same."

John agreed. "Why not? Canada's even bigger than the U.S. and it has one-tenth the population. Seems like you'd get a better deal on real estate up there."

"Hey, our marquee cities, Toronto, Montreal and Vancouver, are plenty expensive and … other than that you might be right."

As Rebecca took a look at the view from the room's windows, John sat in an easy chair and lapsed into a thoughtful silence. Without turning to look at him, Rebecca asked, "That's Puget Sound out there, isn't it?"

"Yes," he said, giving the question only fractional attention.

Rebecca turned and looked at him. "You're deep in thought, huh? Should I wait or ask if it's any of my business?"

John refocused as she took a seat opposite him. "Your comment about Canada following Freddie Strait Arrow's lead made me think maybe the idea wasn't Freddie's at all."

"No? Whose then?" She made the leap, not needing John to answer. "Marlene?"

He nodded.

John had told her of his suspicion that Marlene was Coyote. He'd been ready for the notion to make him the butt of any number of jokes. Still, he'd thought it too important a part of his life not to share with his prospective wife. To his relief, she didn't think she might be marrying a lunatic.

She'd loved reading stories of the supernatural as a girl, and several of them had involved native cultures. For a while, she'd thought she might become a cultural anthropologist, like John's mother. Rebecca thought the shared intellectual affinity was another sign she and John were meant for each other.

That idea was a bit too Oedipal for John to examine closely, but he was glad he'd been forthcoming and his revelation hadn't become a point of ridicule.

"I have something else to tell you about Marlene," he said, "but I'd prefer that you keep it to yourself."

"Something *beyond* her being Coyote? That'd be a little much, wouldn't it?"

"She intends to run for president of the U.S. Not next year, I think, but the cycle after that."

That left Rebecca momentarily speechless. Then she said, "Well, Coyote or not, you've got to admire the woman's ambition. How do you feel about that?"

"Decidedly ambivalent," he told her. "If she took the country's interest to heart, I think she'd run rings around the rest of the world. But Coyote's main and abiding interest is herself. She might take it into mind to work for the repeal of the 22nd Amendment, the one limiting a president to two terms of office. I can imagine her going after Franklin Delano Roosevelt's record, and beating it substantially."

"Well, the obvious counter-move to that is you'd have to run against her."

Despite an attempt to keep a straight face, the corners of Rebecca's mouth turned upward.

That wasn't enough to keep John from shuddering at the thought.

"Much as I love my country," he said, "I don't know if I'd be up to that."

Rebecca moved away from the window and sat on the arm of John's chair, draping an arm around his shoulders. "You'd do it if you had to."

"Maybe if we were well settled into our marriage by then; this country doesn't elect bachelors. And that would mean ..."

"I'd have to migrate south and become a U.S. citizen. I joked with my lawyer about doing as much."

John reached up and put a hand on hers. "You could always visit your family when you felt the need. Canada is right next door."

She nodded. "It'd be an adjustment, but I think I could do it. You know what would bother me the most though, don't you?"

John said, "Yeah, I do. The idea of losing a fight and being exiled from the RCMP."

"Right. Just the thought makes me want to have another go at Serge Marchand."

"Come on now. Leave him the one nut he has."

Rebecca laughed. She kissed John. "You are very good for me."

"Does that mean you'll go trekking the Cascades with me, looking for dangerous characters?"

Rebecca said, "We didn't talk about it yet, but do I get to carry a weapon?"

John nodded. "Sure. I'm not looking for a firefight, but you never know what might happen. If any lowlife gets shot, though, it'd probably be better if I took credit."

"Okay, but if I have to bag a marauding bear or lion, I get to keep the trophy."

"Deal," John said.

— **CHAPTER 12** —

Cascade Mountains — Washington State

As the sun sank in the sky, it took the air temperature down with it. Valeria and Ernesto sat on the ground opposite each other in a clearing with the makings of a large unlit campfire in between them. A resourceful woman, Valeria even had matches with her. Since arriving in the mountains, she'd made a point of buying or filching everything she could from the camp's supplies. She'd amassed quantities of packaged snack food, needles and thread to mend garments, aspirin and other pain-killers the *campesinos* used to extend their hours of toil. She'd thought all of it might be useful, if she and Ernesto ever tried to make an escape from the camp.

She dearly would have loved to pilfer a canteen. That would be just the thing to hold water on a trip through the wilderness. But the only things the workers had to drink from were cheap plastic cups. They cracked easily and were replaced after each communal dinner.

Valeria did manage to buy an extra pair of socks for herself and Ernesto from the meager stipend each worker received on top of his or her debt repayment credit. She also purchased a book of matches from a fellow who smoked, tobacco not marijuana. The workers were not allowed to partake of the crop they grew, processed, guarded and shipped.

Stoners were not known for their diligent work habits.

Valeria's idea of making an escape was more fantasy than

reality. Still, the delusion that her fate was hers to determine made it easier to get through each day. She was unable simply to grind out her time of bondage the way Ernesto did. She had never been a marine.

Not really expecting an opportunity to flee to present itself, all of Valeria's spare food, medicine and even the map she'd drawn from her memory of the trip up into the mountains had been left behind in the corner of the tent in which she and Ernesto had slept. But she kept her matches in her pocket, a talisman as much as objects with the purpose of starting a fire.

So she had the matches with her when Ernesto had been befouled by the stink bomb and she'd been assigned the chore of making him tolerable company again. She knew how the others regarded Ernesto, an oaf with a sad excuse for a mind and no sense of simple good manners much less social graces. Still, he was someone who, beyond all understanding, had won the heart of a beautiful woman.

Ernesto cultivated the misconception of who he was as carefully as the others grew the marijuana. He'd explained himself to Valeria just one time, the day he'd saved her life.

"Better your enemies should think of you as a dwarf not a giant."

She'd wondered if he'd learned that from the marines or his father, but never asked.

Sunshine turned into twilight and Ernesto told his wife, "There is no one nearby, except for maybe that bear. I think if we're careful it will be safe to light our fire now."

Valeria fastened on to the first half of her husband's message. "You really think a bear is following us?"

Ernesto saw she clearly hoped he was playing a joke on her.

To her regret, though, she knew that wasn't his way.

"I haven't seen it yet, but I have heard it. It's too big to be a mountain lion."

Valeria's voice quavered. "Do bears eat people?"

"I imagine they eat whatever they want. Perhaps we shouldn't have washed the stink off ourselves. Then we might have smelled like spoiled food. Something unfit to eat."

"Stop it," she said. "I'm already scared."

"I have my rifle, and that furry fellow is not quiet. He doesn't need to be. He's big, strong, fast and loud. Nothing in this forest is hunting him. But if he comes for us, I will shoot him between his eyes. That will take down any creature, great or small."

"What if you fall asleep?"

"I won't."

"Neither will I."

"Light the fire," Ernesto said. "No one besides the bear will see it."

Valeria needed only one match to get a blaze going. Looking past the flames, she told Ernesto, "I want to sit next to you."

He asked, "If you were sitting next to me, and the bear did come, what would you do?"

"Pray to Jesus to save me."

"*Sí*, but what else?"

"Hold you as tight as I could."

"Exactly. Not a good idea when I'd have to move very fast to get my shot off."

Valeria was too proud to sulk, but she was clearly not happy. "How many nights will we have to spend in this wilderness? I don't think I can take too much of this."

"Other than the bear, and maybe the lions and wolves in these mountains, is there anything else that scares you?" Ernesto asked.

Valeria lifted her chin and shook her head.

Ernesto said, "What worries me is what we'll do when we get *out* of the wilderness. The men who have us peasants grow their marijuana will be looking for us. Even if they don't find us, we will still have to find a way to survive in a new country we have entered illegally."

Valeria stared at her husband through the dancing light of the flames.

"You don't wish to go back to the camp, do you?" She found

that idea hard to believe.

Ernesto said, "I do, but not in the way you think."

"What other way is there?"

"To go not as a *campesino* but as a *ladrón*." A thief.

Valeria didn't understand. "What is there to steal? Bales of marijuana. We could not carry them and run away."

Ernesto shook his head. "The bosses, Julián and that idiot Basilio, have a great deal of money in the camp. They keep it against the day they have to purchase *their* freedom from any gringo police who might find them. I have not seen it, but I know the men who protect it. They say there must be millions of dollars in cash."

That made Valeria stop and think. "Can you take it from them, so much money?"

"I don't know if we can carry it all. I've never seen so much money myself. But we can certainly make off with a lot of it."

"Get out of here and be rich?" Valeria asked. "That would be wonderful. But we'd have to hide from Julián's *compadres* and the bosses in Mexico. Maybe we can go to Canada. That is not so far away."

Ernesto shook his head. "Too cold, colder than here. I am thinking Belize."

They worked out their plans deep into the night.

The bear chose not to bother them, but their empty stomachs growled.

If the bear should make an appearance, maybe they'd eat him.

— CHAPTER 13 —

Saturday, October 17, 2015
The Cascade Loop — Washington State

State Route 20, also known as the Cascade Loop, was a scenic drive that began north of Seattle in Everett, traveled east into the Cascade Mountains and continued into the Columbia River Valley, a district of vineyards and apple groves. John and Rebecca weren't going as far as wine country in their rental Jeep Cherokee, and Rebecca passed up the opportunity to make a joke about John driving a vehicle with a Native American name.

She did, however, make note of a road sign in case John had missed it.

"Cascade Highway 20 closed November to May."

"Yeah, I saw that," John said. "We're on the southern arc of the Loop, but I imagine it can snow pretty hard here, too. Still, we've got two weeks until they close the road."

"Snow never comes early down here in the States?" Rebecca asked.

"I suspect it does, but I've only visited this particular state, never stayed for a prolonged time."

Rebecca glanced out her window. The sky was cloudless, and the thermometer on the dash board reported the outside temperature as being 55 degrees. Neither meteorological condition, the clear sky nor the mild temperature, was particularly comforting. Where she came from, the weather could change dramatically in a matter of minutes.

As if he could read her mind, John said, "Forecast for the rest of the day is okay. After that, things could get a little spotty. A bit of rain, nothing more. No big storm on the horizon."

"Yeah, sure." Rebecca's tone implied that weather forecasts were about as trustworthy as emails from Nigeria.

John didn't miss the skepticism. "Okay, nobody knows what the weather will do, but you'll agree we're pretty well prepared otherwise."

"Well, we certainly have enough firepower," she conceded.

Before heading out of town, they'd stopped at the FBI field office in Seattle to "pick up a rifle or two," as John put it. He'd previously said Rebecca could carry his sidearm.

John introduced his fiancée to Don Mulgrew, the special agent he'd been told to contact. He was happy when Mulgrew extended a hand across the border, so to speak, and told Rebecca, "Always a pleasure to meet someone from an allied service, Lieutenant, especially one of our good friends from Canada."

Rebecca shook his hand and smiled. "Thank you. You're a smooth one, Special Agent."

"My mom and dad raised me right, and my wife keeps me in line."

With the pleasantries concluded, Mulgrew showed John and Rebecca to the armory. It was far larger and better stocked than Rebecca had imagined. The Americans might not have been concerned about hostilities with their northern neighbors, but the FBI was clearly ready to fight off just about anyone else. Even John looked impressed by the array of armaments.

Mulgrew told them, "Word came from DC to give you anything you want in the way of weapons or other necessities."

"From the Acting Secretary of the Interior?" John asked.

Mulgrew nodded. "Her and Vice President Morrissey's chief of staff. You've got important people taking a big interest in you, Mr. Director."

With Marlene's nomination to the cabinet post, John's title had lost its "co-" prefix. He'd also gotten a nice bump in pay. He'd kept the same office since his had a better view than Marlene's old one.

"So what kind of firepower are you looking for, sir?" Mulgrew asked.

John had been asking himself that question since waking that morning.

"I'm thinking something that can suppress enemy fire."

Mulgrew nodded. "Make the fuckers keep their heads down."

"Exactly."

"We can provide an H&K MP5 submachine gun. You ever use one?"

"Back in training at Glynco."

"That'll do, it's one of those things you never forget. Especially when your instruction is first rate. Anything else?"

"A sniper rifle."

Mulgrew said, "I was told to ask no questions, so I'll just say if you're going up into the mountains, I'd recommend an MK14, effective range of 800 yards and rugged as hell."

"Sounds good."

The FBI also outfitted John with ammunition, binoculars, a satellite phone, and a communications package for Rebecca and him including earpieces, microphones and transmitters. The final goodie in the grab-bag was a Buck Rogers night-vision system. Rebecca was surprised by the length and nature of John's shopping list. He'd told her they might encounter bad guys, but now she wondered if she'd signed up for a combat assault unit.

When Mulgrew was done providing John's requests, he politely expressed his regrets to Rebecca. "I'm sorry, Lieutenant, but I wasn't instructed to lend you any firearms. That is, if you wanted any."

Rebecca shook her head, but then had a second thought. "I don't want a gun, but you know what I might like? A bow and a quiver of arrows."

John gave Rebecca a look; Mulgrew gave her a smile.

Then the FBI special agent asked in a mock-serious voice, "Are you qualified on that weapon system, ma'am?"

"I went bow-hunting with my dad for ten years."

"That'll do just fine. I hunt with my father and I have just the thing for you, I think."

He pulled open a drawer beneath a rack of automatic rifles. "This is something I put in the purchase order for myself. When I was asked to justify the expense, I said, 'If you need to take down a bad guy and there's gas in the air, this baby won't ignite it and cause an explosion.' Besides that, the cost was only a few hundred bucks, so they humored me."

Mulgrew took out a black object two feet long and an inch-and-a-half wide. From the sides of the handle he extended two bow limbs made of black fiberglass. "Fully extended, the weapon is 59 inches long, a long bow. Maximum draw weight is 50 pounds. Average arrow speed is 170 feet per second. You put a shot into a living creature, he's going to feel it at the very least. Score a hit in the right spot and you'll have a kill. All that and it weighs just over two pounds."

He extended the weapon to Rebecca and she took it with grin. Mulgrew handed her the bowstring and nodded in approval as she strung the weapon intuitively in the correct manner and removed it as easily. He gave her three 29-inch carbon takedown arrows that each came in two parts and screwed together in the middle for shooting and unscrewed for easy carrying.

He also threw in a knife with a six-inch blade that he said was suitable for filleting any creature that drew a breath. All the weaponry was stored tidily in the back of the Cherokee.

As John pulled into the micro-town of Tesla, population 32, in season, he and Rebecca took notice of their immediate surroundings.

"Cute," she said, looking at the handful of restored Victorian homes and shops on the town's single street, "but where are the locals."

The street was empty and the structures were dark.

"Town's open only part of the year, I was told," John said, "late spring through early autumn. According to Marlene, anyway. She said back in the old days even the native tribe, the Skagits, just spent the summer up here."

"A long-time resort area, huh?" Rebecca asked with a grin.

John nodded and said, "A dot on the map is more like it. I did a little reading while you were bathing last night. Learned that even though we're not very far from Seattle, the terrain up here is so rugged it's still mostly wilderness."

"And Freddie Strait Arrow owns this whole place?"

"That's what I was told, yeah. This hamlet and the two relatively small mountains and intervening valley behind it. The rest of the area is federal land all the way up to Canada."

"Huh," Rebecca said, spotting something new, "so if the town is shut down, where'd that kid come from?" A young man with a camera looped over a shoulder was cautiously edging their way. "He looks a little nervous, doesn't he?"

John said, "Fearful even."

"Maybe I should get out of the car first," Rebecca said.

John replied, "Sure, I'll cover you."

— CHAPTER 14 —

Sierra Madre Occidental — Mexico

In another mountain range, this one south of the Rio Grande, Fausto Zara sat at the head of an ebony table that ran nearly the entire length of his modest home's dining room. The dark wood gleamed; the surrounding walls, painted in a high gloss finish, reflected the light. The table and its equally splendid chairs looked like grandees visiting a poor neighborhood. In another room, a huge platform bed dressed in 1,800 thread count sheets stood as a rebuke to any suggestion of chastity.

Walls had to be taken down to furnish the domicile, but the deluxe interior with the decrepit exterior was the way Zara wanted it. After breaking out of his country's maximum security prison for a third time, having greased the right palms to make his getaway, of course, he had sworn he would never go back. The promise he'd made to himself was buttressed by the federal government's unspoken determination that he would never be captured alive for a fourth time.

Part of the deal for buying his freedom one last time was Zara's promise that he would leave the country immediately and never again make the federal government look like the corrupt fools they were. Zara was supposed to move either south of the Panama Canal or out of the hemisphere entirely. To motivate him toward departing the country, the government had put a huge bounty on his head, if he was brought in dead, but would not pay a *centavo* to anyone who returned him alive. The meaning couldn't have been more clear.

For his part, to facilitate his escape, Zara had said, "Yes, I understand. My time has passed. I must go elsewhere."

Once free, though, he immediately headed for the mountains that were his home, the place he'd long supported with his drug money. Where the people were loyal to him not the government. He immediately began buying weapons in volume. Not just guns but heavy armaments. Surface-to-air missiles. Light anti-tank weapons and, so far, three tanks of his own. If the military came for him, he intended to meet them on equal terms. In truth, if he was able to carry out his plans, Mexico City would need to call in the *yanquis* to win the battle.

That would, of course, paint the government as the puppets of Washington.

And even if he died, his name would become immortal.

Meanwhile, his home was as comfortable as possible and unable to be differentiated from its neighbors by any snooping cameras in the sky above.

Zara smoked as he leafed through a three-ring notebook filled with photos and specs on American attack aircraft. There were so many sleek, deadly flying weapons, it was enough to inspire true awe. He thought if the *yanquis* had his ruthlessness to go with all their weapons they would rule the world. He would certainly be its king, if he could command their arsenal.

The airplane that currently commanded his attention, though, was not a thing of lethal beauty but a heavily armored beast that could absorb much punishment and continue to destroy everything on the ground beneath it. The A-10 Thunderbolt was best known for its brutish appearance and nicknamed the Warthog.

Zara liked that. The aircraft made no pretense to elegant valor. It was just a grunting, snarling creature that devoured everything it fell upon. He felt a kinship with it. The problem until recently was that the *yanquis*, varying from their usual practices, did not sell the Warthog far and wide. The few American allies who possessed them could all be trusted not to sell any out the back door.

That should have been the end of Zara's ambition to start his own air force, except the *yanquis* had decided to retire the Warthog in 2016 and use the savings to pay for yet another sleek new fighter aircraft. The USAF planned to mothball their fleet of A-10s in the American desert of the Southwest and let them slowly decay.

Zara hated that idea the moment he learned of it: To let such magnificent engines of destruction go to waste would be a sin. Sin being a subject on which he was expert. He immediately thought that he must conceive a plan to steal as many Warthogs as he could. Then he was further enraged to learn the retired aircraft would be stripped of their weapons systems.

Cabrónes. That would be like neutering a prize bull. Better to put the animal down.

Then, as if the devil himself had come to Zara's rescue, he learned that Boeing was talking to the Pentagon about buying the Warthogs the *yanquis* no longer had use for and selling them to countries that could appreciate them. The deal had yet to be approved, but Zara knew that in cases where both sides could make money, well, who would be fool enough to do otherwise?

His people were already talking to defense ministers in half-a-dozen countries who would like to become wealthy by acting as purchasing agents for Zara. He could imagine assembling a squadron of A-10s. He was already thinking of where he might build a base for them.

Somewhere out of the way, but within striking distance of Mexico City.

He imagined strafing the presidential palace himself.

Only to take it over soon thereafter.

"You are thinking happy thoughts, *jefe?*"

Zara refocused on the present and saw his second-in-command, Mateo Trujillo, had stepped into the room. Five of Zara's top lieutenants had to lose weight to wedge their way through the over-furnished house. Not Mateo. He was as lean as a whip and as likely to leave scars. His cruelty, though, was functional not sadistic. He did whatever was necessary to complete a job and nothing more. The result was what mattered to him not the process.

Mateo had been recruited from the *Centro de Investigación y Seguridad Nacional*, Mexico's national intelligence service. Part of his education had taken place at Camp Peary in Virginia, better known as The Farm, the CIA's training facility.

Zara nodded and said, "I was about to pray to the Virgin Mother that my airplanes, my Warthogs, get purchased without delay."

"Always good to have faith, *jefe*."

"You're an atheist, Mateo. You told me so."

"I am, yes. Even so, we all have to place our trust somewhere."

Zara had wondered if Mateo might ever try to usurp him. Kill him, that was. Take over his business. He'd even voiced his suspicions to Mateo. His top lieutenant had handed him his gun and calmly said, "Shoot me now, if you are truly concerned."

The boss was about to do just that. Let it be an example to everyone else. Show them nobody lay beyond his judgment. Only Mateo was too damn valuable. He could be counted on to kill enemies who thought they were outside of Zara's reach, and would have been without Mateo. Zara had handed the gun back to Mateo.

"You don't long for power, do you?" Zara had asked.

Mateo had shaken his head. "Being *jefe* is as much a burden as a pleasure."

Looking at Mateo now, Zara saw that a further burden was about to be laid at his feet.

The willingness to be fearlessly honest with him was another of Mateo's virtues.

"You have bad news," Zara said.

Mateo nodded. "Julián called from Washington State. He said he had to relocate the marijuana operation there, the one on the private landholding."

Hearing the details, the man with the camera, the guard who was incompetent with his shooting but nonetheless managed to escape *with* his wife and the need to uproot a productive operation, made Zara glower. He needed every dollar he could get these days. Even used, Warthogs were not cheap.

Starting your own air force was a reach even for a drug lord.

Worse, if the legalization of marijuana was just the beginning of a trend by the *yanquis*, cocaine, amphetamines and even heroin might follow. The fools in Washington, DC might finally start treating the use of drugs as a public health issue not as a crime. If soft drugs were legalized and hard ones were provided free in health clinics, his cartel and all the others would soon be out of business.

What would they do then? Use all their cash to open country clubs for *yanqui* golfers? Tell their killers to become caddies? He knew what he would do in a *sicario's* place if such a day ever came — he'd shoot his *jefe* right between his eyes. Spit on his corpse as well.

Maybe Mateo was right about not wanting to be the boss.

Zara told his second-in-command, "Go north and make things right."

"At any cost, *jefe?*" Mateo asked.

Zara nodded. "*Sí.*"

— CHAPTER 15 —

Cascade Mountains — Washington State

Watching from her hiding spot in the forest at the edge of the meadow, Valeria Batista saw Ernesto become a man completely unlike the one he showed to the rest of the world. He slipped past the tree line and dropped into the high grass leading up to the camp where she'd lived the past four months. In a heartbeat, he was out of sight. She watched for the grass to move, disturbed by the passage of his body. But the wind was blowing just hard enough to cause large swatches of the fine stalks, parched green fading to dull gold, to bend and rebound.

Somewhere out there, Ernesto was working with the wind to camouflage his own disturbance of the grasses. Her husband had left his assault rifle with her, after he was sure she'd understood the rudiments of using the weapon he'd demonstrated for her. He'd taken with him only a long, serrated edge knife she hadn't even known he possessed.

He'd shown it to her and said, "This is a much quieter way to kill."

A chill had run down her spine when she heard that, but it had passed quickly. Why had she married Ernesto? Not only because he'd saved her life, but also because he was kind to her. Because he let her lead their love-making, making her feel wonderfully powerful. But most of all because wherever they went he made her feel safe in a dangerous world.

Now, however, even with the rifle in her hands, she began thinking of the bear again. Both she and Ernesto had heard it as they'd made their way back to the camp from which they'd escaped. They'd planned to observe what was happening there and at least sneak into the tent where they'd slept and reclaim their pitiful few belongings and steal enough water and food to make it out of the mountains.

Ernesto also had his far grander plan: waylay one of the guards he was sure knew where Julián and Basilio kept their big stash of money. If the fellow cooperated, Ernesto would allow him to accompany them and give him a share of the money. If he resisted, Ernesto would slit his throat.

Valeria had suggested an alternative.

"What?" Ernesto asked.

"Besides saying you'll give him some of the money? Tell him I have a sister."

Ernesto laughed. "Yes, we know that one works."

It wasn't that Valeria objected to drastic measures. She just wanted to keep the blood on her husband's hands to a minimum. He really was a good, kind man, and she didn't want his conscience to persuade him otherwise.

Meanwhile, she couldn't help but fear for herself. That damn bear was getting closer. She could feel it. She listened for its approach. Steeling herself, she turned her head to look back the way she and Ernesto had come. Maybe the damn thing was sneaking up behind her.

She strained her eyes to see the creature. It had to be big from the sounds they'd heard. How in the name of God could it hide so perfectly? A loud grunt finally gave its position away. The noise came not from behind her but from ahead. The beast had looped around her.

Valeria spun her head around, the assault rifle coming to her shoulder just as Ernesto had showed her. She looked down the barrel at the iron-framed sight-picture and … that's when she saw the grasses move in a way not caused by the wind or Ernesto.

Something very big pushed them aside, heading not toward her but in the direction of the camp.

The bear was going after Ernesto. Who had only a knife to defend himself.

Forgetting stealth and everything other than the terror she felt for the man she loved, Valeria stepped forward and yelled, "Ernesto! The bear is coming for you!"

As if in anger that its plan had been revealed, the huge animal stood on its hind legs and looked back at Valeria. All but telling her, "You'll be my second meal today, after I eat your chubby husband."

Valeria clicked the rifle's shot selector to automatic and let fly with a long burst of fire.

The recoil was far greater than she had expected and most of the rounds flew harmlessly into the sky, but the first one must have found its mark in some measure. The bear crashed to the ground with a blood-chilling howl of pain, but it wasn't dead. The tall grasses thrashed this way and that.

Valeria couldn't tell if the beast would keep after Ernesto or come for her.

Worse, she'd emptied the entire clip of its ammunition.

She had another, but Ernesto had yet to show her how to reload.

Tesla — Washington State

The young guy with the camera extended a trembling hand and said, "Jesus, I hope you two are the good guys."

John exchanged an impassive look with Rebecca.

She knew what to do. She took the young guy's hand in both of hers and said, "Yeah, we are. Most days, anyhow."

That reassurance proved less than entirely comforting so John added, "I'm a federal officer and the lady is a lieutenant with the Royal Canadian Mounted Police."

Rebecca let the kid's hand go and gave him a salute.

He looked at John and asked, "You're not kidding, are you?"

"Not at all. I'm with the Bureau of Indian Affairs."

Still thinking he might be the victim of a joke, maybe a malicious one, the kid took a step backward. He stopped his retreat when both John and Rebecca produced their IDs. He peered at each of them, and asked, "What is this, some kind of joint operation?"

"Nothing so formal," John said.

Rebecca added, "We're engaged to be married."

"I'm working a case and my fiancée is helping out. A working vacation you might say."

Another look of doubt creased the kid's face but a second look at their credentials allayed that. "Well, that's cool, I guess."

The kid introduced himself as Bruno Bandi. "But everyone calls me Beebs."

"And you're a photographer," Rebecca said.

"Yeah."

John took a closer look at Beebs' camera and the equipment bag dangling from his shoulder to his hip. He asked, "Your camera have Wi-Fi?"

"Sure does," Beebs said.

"You got a long lens in your bag?" John asked.

"Uh-huh."

Rebecca saw what John was getting at.

She asked Beebs, "Did you take a long-distance picture of my sweetie and me and send it off to a cloud somewhere?"

"Several pictures," Beebs admitted.

Rebecca looked back at John. "Kid's pretty slick. If we were bad guys, he'd have sent pictures of his killers off to be retrieved later."

"I almost wet myself walking over here. Those IDs are real, aren't they?"

A slight quaver in Beebs' voice gave the question a tremolo quality.

"Yes, they are," John told Beebs with a pat on his shoulder. "Why don't you tell us what you're doing up here, and maybe we'll tell you a bit about our mission."

Beebs said he was working for Freddie Strait Arrow, doing location photography for a project the "rich dude" had planned. He didn't think he was supposed to talk about that, but he did tell John and Rebecca about the guy who shot at him, and how he'd responded.

"Mexican, you say?" John asked. "Any chance he could have been Native American?"

Beebs thought about that. "Might've been, partly, but to me he looked like a lot of people I've seen down on Olvera Street in L.A. New to the country. Hadn't had much time to assimilate. No tats that I could see and his clothes didn't look American."

"Okay, that's a pretty good eye you had for someone under fire," John said.

Beebs shrugged. "A good eye is the first thing you need to shoot good pictures."

"But the guy who was shooting at you, his eye wasn't so good?" Rebecca asked.

Beebs took a moment to answer. "I've been thinking about that. He probably wasn't all that far away when he took his first shot. It was almost like he missed on purpose, but I can't think why he'd do that, if he was going to shoot at all."

John said, "Maybe he only wanted to scare you."

"At least until you stink-bombed him," Rebecca added.

Beebs nodded. "Yeah, I tried not to give him another chance after that."

"Are we the first people you've had contact with?" John asked.

"Yeah, to talk to. I lost my phone in the woods, but I wrote a message on a blackboard in the house I've been using. Took a photo and sent it off to the cloud."

"That's good thinking," John said.

He was about to ask another question when he heard something in the distance. He turned and looked at Rebecca. She nodded. "I heard it, too."

Beebs said, "That was gunfire." Certainty in his voice.

"Was that what the rifle firing at you sounded like?" John

asked.

"Yeah, but a lot louder and one at a time, not all in a bunch at once. What the hell is going on around here?"

"Without giving away any secrets," John said, "that's what we're here to find out. You know if there's a place we can put our car? Somewhere off the street."

Beebs nodded. "The garage behind the house I'm using has an extra slot."

CHAPTER 16

Dulles Toll Road — Sterling, Virginia

Freddie Strait Arrow and Marlene Flower Moon rode in the back of his limo on their way to Washington Dulles International Airport. Freddie had read the chalkboard message Beebs had sent to his private online message board. The poor guy had been shot at and almost killed? Jeez. Freddie had never imagined things would get that scary.

Yeah, sure, he'd sent Beebs out into the woods where, he'd been told, people were growing weed on his land but, damn, wasn't marijuana supped to make you mellow? Laid back and laughing at the world. That's what he'd always heard. He'd never used the stuff, not even in brownies or candy. Hadn't ever done any drugs at all, not even alcohol.

Mom and Dad had warned him about that, having a possible genetic predisposition to not handle booze well at all. He'd heeded their warning. Didn't really need any pharmaceuticals to get him off. Freddie got high on math. Making numbers dance to the tune he called was his thing.

That and now sex with Marlene.

After reading the message from Beebs over Freddie's shoulder, Marlene had said, "That's not good, but Tall Wolf will take care of it."

"Me, too," Freddie replied, getting to his feet.

"You want to go where there's gunfire?"

She wasn't criticizing him, merely searching his eyes to see if she'd overlooked a building block of his character.

"I want to see Beebs, tell him I'm sorry about what happened, find a way to show my gratitude that he's all right. See if there's a spot in my company for him, if he's interested. I mean, it was pretty damn cool, a guy using a stink bomb to fight off a bastard with a rifle."

Marlene conceded the point. "That was imaginative, but you're thinking about more than a lucky photographer. The situation has become personal for you."

Besides the physical pleasure she brought him, Freddie delighted in how well Marlene could read him. Like many math and science guys, understanding his fellow man — or woman — was not his strong suit. Sometimes she had a fix on his emotions before he did.

That could be scary but it was also kind of comforting, as long as they were happy with each other. The situation being conditional was something even he understood.

"Yeah, you're right."

Marlene told him, "You've seen the scar on my chest."

Freddie had but he'd had neither the nerve nor the bad manners to ask about it.

He only nodded now.

Marlene told him, "It came from a bullet shot from a rifle. I was very lucky. Not many people would have survived my kind of wound."

To his unspoken shame, Freddie found her fortitude sexy.

That a woman who could spit in death's eye had chosen him.

"I'm glad you did," he said.

Marlene caressed his cheek, but stayed on point. "What I'm saying is *you* might not survive such a trauma."

Freddie had to stop and think about that. Which he did at his usual warp speed. The idea of dying had already occurred to him, of course, and was quickly tossed away like a gum wrapper, the way any healthy guy in his twenties would discard it. Freddie knew, with his new microchip design, he had already left a positive and significant mark on the world.

The papers in his vault, in and of themselves, would contribute to further advances.

So in terms of creating a personal memorial he was good.

His name and his work would be remembered.

Only with the arrival of Marlene did he pause to consider that there might be a whole lot of new people out there in the world he'd like to meet. That would require staying alive, but winning the approval of such people, gaining their friendship and maybe even their love, that wouldn't happen if he lived his life meekly. Taking the safer path whenever the road branched wouldn't get him to where he wanted to go.

So Freddie told Marlene, "I won't make Ronald Reagan's mistake."

"What?" Marlene asked.

"I won't forget to duck," he told her.

And with that they were off to the airport.

Having lent his personal aircraft to John Tall Wolf, he'd had to call ahead and arrange for another plane to carry Marlene and him to Washington State. The discussion between Freddie and the person he'd described as his fix-it guy hadn't taken a minute. No run-of-the-mill executive jet had been available on such short notice, but a customized Boeing 737 was on hand for what Freddie had described as "a few more bucks."

Marlene was impressed that Freddie never preened about his ability to throw huge sums of money around like they were pocket change. His ego didn't rest on his money. He exulted in his ability to solve problems that defeated other computer engineers and scientists. He also took a deep and newfound interest in the erotic possibilities two people might explore.

That would pale eventually, Marlene knew, but in the meantime she intended to create a wellspring of enduring affection for her in Freddie's heart. Whenever she needed him, he would be there for her. Whether she needed money or something else.

What that meant, of course, was Marlene would have to keep Freddie alive.

If, or more likely when, any hostilities began.

CHAPTER 17

Cascade Mountains — Washington State

Valeria Batista stood her ground as the creature charged through the tall grass in her direction. Not knowing how to reload the rifle, she had no recourse other than to seize the weapon's stubby barrel in both hands and hold it like a baseball bat. She would have laughed, had she seen anyone else do this. As a gesture of futility, she couldn't imagine anything more ridiculous.

Nonetheless, if she was about to die she would do so fighting until the end. Before some monstrous agony was inflicted upon her, she would do her best to mete out a measure of pain to the beast she was sure would tear her limb from limb. If she got really lucky, she might slam the rifle's butt into one of the bear's eyes. Send him careening in another direction, never knowing how he'd become the one to suffer, but not daring to take another chance of worse to come.

Valeria began taking deep breaths, charging her muscles for the literal fight of her life. She heard the bear's furious growls grow louder as it sprinted closer. She forced her knees not to buckle ... and then she heard another blood-curdling sound. This new uproar also held the note of a growl but it was far more than that. Mixed with the blast of immense fury was a chain of keening distress.

The bear broke from the grass no more than twenty feet from Valeria. The animal was bleeding freely from the top of its front left leg. It glared with rage at Valeria, as if it understood who had caused its pain. But the bear, a huge grizzly she could now see, came to an abrupt stop and turned its head toward the sound of the howling thing coming up fast behind it.

It had no frame of reference for any creature acting as an aggressor.

That was when Valeria finally recognized the call of the pursuing stalker. It was Ernesto's voice, given the power and ferocity of a man racing to sacrifice his own life to save hers. That left only one thing for her to do. She glared at the animal, bent forward at the waist, thrust her head out farther still, bared her teeth and screamed with all the strength in her body.

The bear turned to look at her and then looked back to see whatever was coming up from behind. Valeria managed to raise the volume of her own furious scream. The bear became confused over which threat to confront first. In the end, it acted on instinct.

It ran toward Valeria and when it was ten feet from her it broke sharply to its right and ran into the woods. Its former prey also reacted instinctively. Valeria found a stone at her feet, scooped it up and hurled it at the retreating animal. The projectile caught the bear on its hindquarters, spurring it to a howl of pain and greater speed.

When Valeria turned to look for Ernesto, he was right there, not six inches from her, his knife in his right hand and somehow the rifle he'd already taken from her in his left. He put the knife away and laid a gentle hand on her shoulder. "You are unharmed?"

Unable to find her voice, she only nodded. Tears rolled down her cheeks.

"Thank you for calling out your warning to me," Ernesto said. "That was a very brave thing to do. Did you hit the animal at all with your gunfire?"

She nodded again and her chin firmed up. "I did. Just once, I think."

"That was enough for now. May I have the other magazine, please?"

She reached into a pocket and handed it to him.

He ejected the empty clip and seated the full one in the weapon. They were rearmed.

Ernesto told her, "We will have to be careful. The bear is frightened but not yet dead." Before Valeria could dwell on that, he added, "Come, let me show you what I've found in the camp."

John and Rebecca heard the growl of a large, fast approaching animal.

"Bear," Rebecca said.

John nodded. "Big one. Probably a grizzly. Go with the MK14, not the bow."

"Yeah, my thought, too."

For his part, John raised the barrel of the H&K MP5 submachine gun. Instinctively, they stood back to back, giving themselves a 360-degree field of fire. Except for all the damn trees in the way. When you were making your way up the slope of a forested mountain, having trees as obstacles was just part of the challenge. The situation became considerably more difficult, though, when an apex predator, possibly weighing as much as 800 pounds, was darting between the conifers and maples, maybe coming right your way. It made for a hair-raising circumstance.

Especially when the clamor of the charging animal had been preceded by a burst of fire from an automatic weapon and punctuated by an animal bellow of pain. All of which had happened fairly damn close. With the animal getting closer by the second.

"Someone shot the bear?" Rebecca asked.

"Sounded like it," John answered. "Maybe with an AR-15. Doesn't seem to have slowed it down much, though."

Further speculation about the bear was cut off by two human voices, male and female, their voices clearly cutting through the trees and speaking Spanish.

"You've got some strange damn campers in this country," Rebecca told John.

"Place hasn't been the same since 1492," he admitted.

There was no time for further wisecracks as something massive and brown flashed past them, never bothering to spare them a glance. John and Rebecca scarcely had the time to turn their heads and see it. A collective chill ran down the spines they pressed closer together.

"Damn, that thing was big, and fast as hell," Rebecca said.

"Faster than a race horse for a short burst is what I've been told," John replied, "and that specimen was running on a bum leg."

"What?"

"You didn't see it? It was bleeding from its front left leg, up near where the leg joins the scapula. At least one of the shots we heard must have hit it."

"Great. So now we have a *wounded* grizzly wandering around nearby."

"Looks like it. The beast might take out its hard feelings on anyone who's handy, too, not just the SOB who shot it. Speaking of which, we've got another worry: Someone else in the woods is also packing an automatic weapon."

"Yeah, shit, and I thought I was in trouble back home."

"So you don't think we'll look back on this and laugh, tell our kids how tough Mom and Dad are?"

"Maybe if the bear bleeds out and we turn him into a rug."

John smiled. You had to admire a woman who could keep her sense of humor in a tough spot. He did anyway. "I think brother bear is probably still putting distance between us and him. We ought to move on. Avoid the Spanish-speaking bear hunters for the time being and see what's happening at the coordinates Marlene gave me."

"Really? You don't want to call for backup?"

"We'll be careful. If it's just human beings with firearms up ahead, well, hell, that's not going to daunt a Mountie, is it?"

"You never know," Rebecca said, "I might get my walking papers at the worst possible moment."

John nodded. "Could happen that way. Then we'll just have to see what *I'm* made of."

CHAPTER 18

10,000 Feet and Climbing above Culiacan, Mexico

Civil aviation aircraft flying from Mexico to the United States had to follow strict security protocols. The Electronic Advance Passenger Information System required traveler manifest information for each person aboard, notice of arrival information and notice of departure information. All of this data had to be received by U.S. Customs and Border Patrol at least sixty minutes before takeoff, for both flights arriving in the United States and departing from the country.

The U.S Air Defense Identification Zone worked to identify all aircraft in the vicinity of the country's airspace boundaries, especially inbound flights. Ever since 9-11, the federal government took the responsibility of identifying and monitoring incoming passenger flights very seriously. An aircraft that hadn't filed a proper flight plan would be met by fighter jets authorized to shoot down the intruder if necessary.

Despite his employment by a fugitive drug lord, Mateo Trujillo had no trouble gaining prompt clearance for the Dassault Falcon that would carry him to Seattle. In part, that was due to his continuing role as a "consultant" with his country's *Centro de Investigación y Seguridad Nacional*. As to working for Fausto Zara, well, that was a discreet omission on his official list of legitimate private sector clients.

There were those south of the Rio Grande who knew his dirty

little secret, of course, but they had their own thumbs in any number of purloined pies. Indeed, there were some companies who hired him *because* he'd shown he could work profitably with a man as dangerous as Zara. Having Mateo on the payroll was a winking admission that he could put in a fix with the highest levels of the national government.

Little of that, however, was what gave him easy access to the U.S.

When the Falcon reached its cruising altitude, Mateo Trujillo made a phone call across the breadth of North America to Virginia. It needed to ring only once before it was answered. A woman's voice said, *"Liebchen."* Sweetheart.

Mateo knew the flight crew and the cabin attendant had a command of Spanish, Portuguese, English and even French between them. Unless one of the bastards had secretly been studying German, though, he would be safe.

He used the language in which he'd been addressed. He also continued the ruse that the call was romantic in nature, listening for any hint of friendly laughter coming from the area of the cockpit. Not hearing any, he got down to business.

"I'm coming north. I might need to kill someone. I trust clean-up help will be available if I need it."

"Who's going to die?" the woman asked.

"An underling of Zara's. Maybe two."

"We can live with that, if you're not too gaudy about it."

"I'll take your sensibilities into account."

"Good. Make time for a little chat with me before you go back home."

"I plan to. I might not be going back."

"Oh, my, are things getting that bad? Should I bring candy and flowers?"

Mateo was the one to laugh now, only there was nothing romantic to the sound.

"Just bring the severance package I signed on for." He broke the connection.

Neither Mateo nor the CIA had let the opportunity to establish a working relationship pass them by when he'd come to train at The Farm. He'd been their inside man with Zara's operation for years. He'd provided small tips to the U.S. that implicated his rivals in Zara's cartel with betraying the boss. The result was meaningless "victories" in the war on drugs. That and the elimination of Mateo's competition, hastening his rise within the organization.

Now, he was going to cash out.

In more ways than the CIA knew.

CHAPTER 19

Cascade Mountains — Washington State

M eat," Valeria said. She looked at several stacks of plastic-wrapped cuts of beef in a freezer that was no longer connected to a gas-powered generator. "This is beef, isn't it?"

Her spoken English was passable; her reading of the language lagged behind. She couldn't decipher the labels on the packages of meat.

Ernesto's foreign language literacy was more advanced. He'd studied *inglés* in the military in hopes of advancement. "These packages contain the finest cut of beef, what they call filet mignon. It is supposed to melt in your mouth."

"Like ice cream?"

Ernesto laughed. "I truly don't know, but that's an interesting thought. How much beef have we eaten here?"

"None. We eat chicken. We get enough to eat but it's always chicken."

"So who must eat the beef around here, then?"

"Julián and that pig Basilio."

"*Sí*, and why would they leave this wonderful meat behind?"

That question was easy to answer. "Because they did not take the freezer and it would spoil."

"Exactly. They were in a big hurry and the freezer is heavy. It would be a burden in any case, and especially so if they had to climb a mountain with it."

"Why would they have to do that?"

Ernesto explained that he'd learned of the other sites where the growing and processing operation might move if circumstances so dictated.

"How did you do that?" Valeria asked.

"I pretended to be asleep when Eusebio and Chucho were talking one night." Those men were the captain of the guards and his number two. "They never suspected simple-minded Ernesto might be listening to them. I may have pretended to snore a little."

Valeria smiled in appreciation, and silently told herself never to underestimate her husband.

"So what do we do now?" she asked.

"Well, we have the food and water we need to get out of these mountains. I've learned some people actually like to eat beef raw. But others say that can make you sick. So our challenge is to think of a way for you to cook the meat that won't draw that bear or any of his animal friends to our fiesta."

The very thought frightened Valeria. "I'd rather eat chicken from a can."

"I found some other things," Ernesto told her.

He took four fully loaded ammunition magazines out of his pockets.

"We could kill quite a few bears now, if we needed to. Or we could let them eat my cooking. That would surely be the end of them."

Valeria laughed. Ernesto had told her he was the worst cook in the world. She'd accepted that at first. Now, she thought he probably did that as well as he did everything else. But she was smart enough to play along.

"I will cook and you will watch for bears."

"*Bueno,* but there is one more thing to think about. Where does our future lie? I told you the story about Julián having a lot of money up here."

"*Sí.*"

"I know now that it's more than just a story."

He reached in a pocket and took out a hundred dollar bill. The middle of the note looked like it had been stepped on by a dirty boot but the edges were crisp and clean. Ernesto handed it to Valeria.

"For you, *querida*." Dear.

She took it and set to brushing off the dirt. Then she looked at her husband.

"Is it real?"

He nodded. He'd seen many such portraits of Benjamin Franklin when the marines raided the narcos. "Do you think it belongs to one of the workers or guards?"

She shook her head. "Neither."

"So it must belong to one of our bosses then."

"It might be the only one, this *cien dolares*." Hundred dollars.

Ernesto shook his head.

"Tell me," he said. "If you had just that one bank note, would you search for it until you found it?"

Valeria nodded.

"But if you had more money than you could count, how hard would you look?"

Valeria got the point. "Not at all. So what do we do?"

Ernesto said, "We must agree, of course, but I think we should find out if God means for us to become rich."

CHAPTER 20

Ottawa, Ontario — Canada

Jules Marchand was one of 58 chief superintendents in the RCMP. His rise through the force's hierarchy had been both steady and relatively swift. Still, he had all of his equally ranked colleagues and another 33 assistant and deputy commissioners to leapfrog if he wanted to reach his ultimate goal of becoming commissioner of the whole shooting match.

He'd carefully analyzed the dozens of men and a handful of women equal to or above him in rank. He knew their ages, strengths, weaknesses and dirty little secrets. Sifting out the ones who'd retire before ever reaching the top, the ones whose records didn't match his own, the ones he could expose or subtly black-mail, he figured his real competition numbered two men and perhaps one woman.

The woman was Deputy Commissioner Eileen Murphy, who was currently sitting in judgment of Jules' nephew, Sergeant Serge Marchand. One of the two men he viewed as real competition was Chief Superintendent Edward Bramley, who was both Rebecca Bramley's uncle and her godfather. That SOB also had the top job in his sights.

Based on their records in the RCMP, it might take a coin-flip to decide which man would take the top spot, unless a wave of political correctness and women's rights swept them both aside for Eileen Murphy. Not long ago the very thought of a woman leading the force would have been laughable.

Then the damn Americans had to elect Patricia Grant president, and it looked as if they might follow her with another woman, Vice President Jean Morrissey. More Canadians than Jules Marchand cared to think about loved both American women. Morrissey was at least a first-rate hockey player for her gender, but damn them both.

If there was one thing that made Canadians truly uneasy about Americans it was the idea that the U.S. might outstrip its neighbor in matters of social progress. Given its small, sensible population, Canada was supposed to blaze that trail.

Americans were supposed to see the northern light and follow. But now ...

Merde. Shit.

There was a chance that Murphy might beat out both him and Bramley. He certainly couldn't try to muscle Murphy into punishing Rebecca Bramley and promoting Serge. Not that there was any promotion that truly compensated a man for losing half his manhood. Sure, there was any number of things men said they would give their left nut for, but not really.

Jules certainly wouldn't.

"You are feeling regret about your nephew's predicament, Jules?"

Chief Superintendent Marchand was dining at the Capital Club with Deputy Minister of Public Safety Canada — *Sécurité Publique Canada* — Theo Blanchet. The RCMP fell under Public Safety's purview. Dinner had been served and there wasn't another soul within thirty feet of them.

Jules sipped his wine. "Personally, I can't stand the bastard. He's a dolt. Perhaps losing a testicle will be just the thing he needs to start thinking above the belt instead of below it."

"Is he as bad as all that?"

Jules refilled his glass and topped off Blanchet's.

"If anyone other than a Bramley had caused his troubles, I would let Serge suffer whatever cruelty Eileen Murphy chooses to inflict upon him. But there is the larger Marchand family to think about. They all expect me to defend our name, and I do love my youngest brother, Serge's father. Except for Marcel's blindness to his son's flaws, he's a fine man."

"So you invited me to dinner to ask for my counsel, help or both?" Blanchet asked.

Jules sighed. "At the risk of spoiling your appetite, old friend, I'd like to know if you can stomach the idea I've already settled on."

Blanchet shrugged. "There's very little that can put me off my feed. Whatever your notion is, of course, I'll have to be able to sell it to the minister."

The number two man in Public Safety Canada had one final bureaucratic step to climb himself. He'd just told Jules that his idea would have to be politically acceptable, not just to the minister, really, but to the public as well.

The story of the contretemps between Rebecca Bramley and Serge Marchand had broken as a national news story just that morning, becoming something of a sensation. The population at large was taking sides, with a slight edge going to Bramley. Jules thought that showed both female solidarity and an unfortunate number of men who lived under their wives' thumbs.

The Bramleys, no doubt under the leadership of Chief Superintendent Edward Bramley, must have taken the story public. The Bramleys didn't have the same number of highly placed political friends that the Marchands did. So they'd decided to enlist public opinion on their side. The gambit was well played, and Jules knew he couldn't afford to underestimate Bramley in the future as both of them lunged for the commissioner's job.

"I understand completely, Theo," Jules told the deputy minister. "My thinking is both Serge and the Bramley woman get posted somewhere cold and remote."

"But not together."

"Of course not. At opposite ends of the Arctic Ocean but equally near the North Pole."

Blanchet smiled. "Where they can both develop a taste for

whale blubber."

"Do the Inuit still consume that?" Jules asked.

"They do. I was up there last summer. Had some. Not to my taste at all, but the roast caribou wasn't bad. Of course, the natives have what they call southern food, too. Better known to you and me as fast food. We truck it up there, you know."

Jules shook his head. "I didn't. I assume the winter nights are still long and cold, and there's little first-rate theater or cinema available."

"Yes, I'm sure you're right about all that," Blanchet said. "So we send both parties, your nephew and Lieutenant Bramley, to hardship posts, and —"

"You know what happens next, old friend," Jules said.

Blanchet nodded. "Once public interest has faded, Serge will make a far quicker return to more settled and civilized locales than the Bramley girl, who will linger in the far north until —"

"She quits," Jules said, "or freezes her ass off."

"I'm sure I can manage that for you," the deputy minister said.

The two men smiled at the reasonableness of their plan.

They toasted each other and finished off the bottle.

CHAPTER 21

Cascade Mountains — Washington State

John and Rebecca circumnavigated their way to the far side of the former illicit pot processing camp. Using their Garmin eTrex20x device that offered a choice of topographical maps or satellite imagery, they picked their way along an indirect path through the forest that John thought would be the safest, i.e. the sneakiest, way to approach the camp without taking them too far afield. The waited on the periphery of the cleared area, concealed by trees, watching and listening for signs of life.

John held the MP5 submachine gun in his hands. He was relaxed but he had the weapon's safety off. Rebecca held her bow, its limbs extended and strung, in her left hand, an arrow in her right hand. John's weapon was intended for a quick kill, if things came to that; Rebecca's bow was meant for a quiet kill or a debilitating wound, depending on the situation. She'd assured John she was up to taking either kind of action. Provided their own lives were in jeopardy.

"Didn't really think things would come to this," John whispered. "Still hope it won't."

"Me, too. If we *have* to shoot at people, so be it. But if that bear comes looking for us, I'm pretty sure my three arrows aren't going to stop him, try as I might."

Keeping a straight face, John said, "Pretend the bear is Serge Marchand."

She laughed quietly. "Yeah, that'd be good motivation." Then she understood John's subtext and gave him a light sock on the shoulder. "You meant I should put an arrow in the bear's nut-sack, didn't you?"

"Well, if it's a male and he stands on his hind legs, gives you a clear shot."

Rebecca grinned. "Yeah, I imagine even a big grizzly wouldn't be able to shrug off something like that."

"Just a thought," John said.

After waiting thirty minutes, John said, "You think the place is empty? I do."

"Me, too."

"Ready to check things out?'

She nodded, but said, "Should we call in first? Let Madam Secretary know we've arrived and are going in with weapons at the ready?"

John gave it a moment's thought and nodded. "I'll send a text to Marlene."

He did so and kept his phone on vibrate so any response wouldn't give away his position.

John asked, "You want to switch from the bow to the MK14?" The sniper rifle.

Rebecca shook her head. "You've put me in an archery frame of mind."

Holding more fire-power and possessing a politically incorrect sense of gallantry, John went first, silently walking point as Rebecca gave him a ten pace lead and then followed. John kept his eyes face front, taking in a visual sweep of 180°, but he was listening a full three-sixty. It pleased him that he couldn't hear Rebecca bringing up the rear. Couldn't smell her either because she was downwind of him. Still, without the benefit of any of the usual five senses, he knew she was behind him, not crowding him but a healthy distance back.

Maybe healthy. An automatic weapon in the hands of a bad guy could spray a long arc of fire in a heartbeat. That was the whole point of such firearms. Still, there would be some small interval in which Rebecca might react if John was targeted first, and a fit person could move a surprising distance in a second or less.

Even so, he thought, this was a hell of a situation in which to put your betrothed.

Rebecca thought so, too. She had an arrow on the bowstring now, ready to draw and let fly. She was doing her best not to watch John; he'd take care of himself and her against any threat in their direction of travel. That was his job.

Hers was to spot any armed dudes — or dudettes — to their right or left, and listen for anyone trying to sneak up on them from behind. Doing all that should have commanded her full attention, but the best she could assign the task was maybe ninety percent. A small, nagging thought kept intruding.

Well, maybe not so small, but definitely persistent. If she put an arrow or three through the gizzard of anyone who didn't walk around on four paws, how was that going to look to Deputy Commissioner Murphy? Like maybe she was the loose cannon in the Bramley vs. Marchand brouhaha? Might the official judgment then become that she'd had every right to, say, sock Marchand on his jaw, but kicking him the way she'd done was the proverbial low blow?

If that was the case, the boom would be lowered on her and Marchand might get off with a slap on the wrist. He might even be encouraged to sue her for … what? She wasn't sure but she thought a guy could both get it up and father a child with just one testicle. Still, explaining to a new sweetheart that you didn't come fully equipped might be dismaying.

Marchand might file a legal action for emotional discomfiture.

Or, if he couldn't get hard, loss of standing.

A soft whistle, sounding like a lark but also like John, brought Rebecca to an abrupt halt. She saw that she'd halved the distance between herself and him, and John was standing before a good sized tent with a door-flap drawn back. An inclination of his head toward his far shoulder drew her to him.

She silently mouthed the word, "Sorry."

He gave a small nod and directed his eyes at the interior of the tent.

Rebecca looked that way. She saw, among other things, two camp beds with aluminum frames, thick memory-foam mattresses and plump pillows. Each bed was covered with a striped wool blanket, the kind advertised as wind resistant and water repellent. Somebody liked a good night's sleep in the woods and was willing to pay top dollar for their comfort.

Speaking of money, a waist-high safe sat at the far end of the tent between the beds. The thing looked like it might weigh a ton, several hundred pounds at least. The door to the strong box stood open and the interior showed empty.

Rebecca took another look at the two beds. The one on her right was neatly made; the one on the left was a jumble. She turned to John trying to understand what had caught his attention. He pointed to the messy bed, before turning to keep an eye on their surroundings.

It took a moment, but Rebecca spotted what had roused John's interest.

Peeking out from beneath the pillow on the unkempt bed was the corner of a wallet. Someone liked to sleep on his boodle. A not inconsiderable sum either. She could see the wallet was thick with American cash. At the exchange rate with the Canadian dollar, that put a 33% premium on every buck there, too.

Rebecca whispered to John, "Farming pays pretty well in your country."

"Even without crop subsidies sometimes," John agreed.

They carefully moved away from the tent and checked out the remainder of the camp. There were odds and ends of all sorts: other tents, big multi-person shelters; numerous black plastic bags that smelled of discarded food; even an unpowered freezer with beef inside; two huge plastic bins filled with bottles of ibuprofen and other NSAIDs and so many items of worn and ragged clothing they didn't bother to count them all.

They didn't find so much as an ounce of marijuana, though. John commented on that once they'd made sure the place had been abandoned.

"Plenty of signs of a vanished civilization," he said, "but no dope at all."

"If you've got to make a quick getaway," Rebecca said, "you take what you value most."

"Right. The marijuana and the people who grew it. They can always grow more. But I don't think anyone knew we were coming, so what scared them off?" John asked.

"Beebs Bandi and his camera?"

John frowned. "Maybe, but the people running this place didn't know of his connection to Freddie Strait Arrow or Freddie's relationship to Marlene. For all they knew Beebs was just a guy with a camera who was lucky to get away and wouldn't ever bother them again."

"We heard an automatic weapon fire and a man and a woman speaking Spanish," Rebecca said. "Maybe they have something to do with the evacuation here."

John nodded. "Maybe. Something certainly scared the bosses, one of them taking off and leaving his wallet behind."

"Leaving all this food here," Rebecca said, "that had to be what drew the bear this way."

"Yeah, and if he's not hurt too bad, he'll be back. If not him, his family and friends will certainly stop by for a nosh."

Rebecca frowned. "Let's not stick around in case they prefer fresh food, like you and me."

"Good point. If we want to call it a day, we've already discovered that somebody was camping out illegally on Freddie's land, and that's what I was asked to do. We could head back to Tesla, get our rental Cherokee and go somewhere with more amenities. Sort out our future."

Rebecca studied John's face. She knew he'd do just what he said, if that was what she wanted. He'd turn the pursuit of the drug operation over to someone else. Maybe the DEA. All she had to do was say, "Let's go."

Instead, she asked, "Is that what you want to do? That'd be fine with me. But if you want to find out what's going on here, I'd be good with that, too."

John told her, "I really couldn't ask you to help me any more, unless you allow me to help you with your problem."

Sounded like they were married already, negotiating terms and conditions.

"Would you really involve your president?"

"Only if I had to. If that was the case, though, yeah, I would."

Rebecca leaned forward and kissed John.

"Let's check out that wallet somebody left behind," he said.

They returned to the tent in question, finding forty one-hundred-dollar bills and two photographs in the wallet.

Polaroids yet. Someone was truly old school.

The first picture showed a large, grinning Hispanic man with two naked ladies nestled under each of his outstretched arms. Each of the women was cupping her breasts and smiling widely for the camera.

"Family reunion?" John asked.

Rebecca shook her head. "Not even if it's the Addams family."

The second photo was a candid head-and-shoulders shot of a clothed Latina woman.

"Much prettier woman," Rebecca said, "but it looks to me like she doesn't know the creep took the picture."

"Quite possibly," John said.

There was no identification in the wallet as to who owned it.

Well, maybe the photos would help provide names.

They stepped out of the tent. John had a text reply from Marlene. He read it and called her.

Rebecca stood watch, looking for bears and cradling the MP5.

Julián Fortuna sat on the ground with his back against a fallen tree trunk. He used a sleeping bag to cushion both his back and his ass, but the damn ground was so cold he could feel it right through the bag and his jeans. He knew for sure it was going to get a lot colder and more uncomfortable after the sun went down.

He already had the *campesinos* clearing the ground needed to set up the new camp. It was hard work and everyone was tired from the uphill trek. There might actually have been mumbles of complaint, despite the guards being in a bad mood of their own and looking like shooting somebody might raise their spirits, except Julián stepped forward to head off trouble with a bit of enlightened and devious management.

He'd told the assembled workers, "We have all had a hard day. So tomorrow will be a day of rest and will not extend your release date. In fact, I will need volunteers to go back down the mountain to retrieve the things we left behind that will make our lives much more comfortable up here. This chore should take no more than a few days, but I will count the time as a month's credit toward an early release."

That news brought a harvest of smiles and excited murmurings.

"I will leave it to you to decide who should earn this bonus," Julián said. "I think a dozen good men will be all I need."

At a stroke, he'd given them positive motivation and pitted them one against another as to who would get to claim his generous offer. Their competition against each other would deflect any hard feelings they'd otherwise direct at him. He was sure his B-school profs would be proud.

As to getting them to continue clearing ground after their difficult journey, Julián said, "*Compañeros,* we will all be much more comfortable tonight if we have the room to build fires without setting the whole forest on fire and making ourselves look like burnt *frijoles.*"

Self-interest was always good motivation, too.

The grumbling subsided and most of the *campesinos* started thinking of how they could be among the ones who would win early release. Showing *el jefe* how hard they could work at that very moment would be a good start. With the potential rebellion peacefully quelled, Julián had turned his attention elsewhere.

As he sat propped against the fallen tree trunk, he used his satellite phone, an Inmarsat BGAN, to create a Wi-Fi hot spot for his MacBook. Deep in the wilds of the Cascade Mountains, he had Internet connectivity. A man who couldn't tap global resources, he'd been taught, might as well be a troglodyte.

Julián had decided in his hour of distress that it might be smart to learn more about his unwitting host, Frederic Strait. He'd always imagined Strait as a bloated old coupon-clipper with liver spotted hands, or possibly a spoiled brat, someone concerned with nothing more than running through his inheritance as fast he could. Racing to see whether his money or his time on earth ran out first.

The way things were going lately, he thought it wise to verify his preconceptions.

Turned out, a Google search told him, he couldn't have been more wrong about Strait.

The guy was now known as Freddie Strait Arrow. Had made billions on his own. Was maybe on his way to becoming the richest man in the world. Damn, Julián thought, the trouble you got into when you didn't do your homework.

That was a lesson you learned in elementary school not B-school.

"Jesus," he said, using the English pronunciation as he continued to read, "I never should have messed with this dude."

Julián hadn't noticed his cousin approach.

Basilio stood over him and asked, "Messed with what dude? Someone I should kill?"

CHAPTER 22

Approaching Tesla — Washington State

The Boeing 737 that Freddie Strait Arrow had chartered had a top cruising speed of 472 knots or 543 miles per hour. Facing little to no headwind on a calm day, and the pilot putting the pedal to the metal, the flight from DC to Seattle had been relatively quick. True, following Federal Aviation Administration rules, the aircraft had to slow to 250 knots as it entered the busy airspace around Seattle-Tacoma International Airport. And it had to slow further for its approach and landing as both the rules and common sense dictated.

But the billionaire's aircraft, with a prospective member of the president's cabinet aboard, didn't have to queue up for landing and circle the airport. It went straight in. Further aiding Freddie and Marlene's intention to get to Tesla as soon as possible, a Sikorsky S-76C executive helicopter was waiting for them. Eliminating the need to get bogged down in automotive traffic. The Sikorsky could do 178 mph.

Freddie and Marlene were nine minutes out from Tesla when Acting Madam Secretary received a call from John Tall Wolf. She put it on speaker so Freddie could participate.

John told them, "We found the camp but not the campers."

"What about the drugs?" Freddie asked. "Were they growing marijuana?"

"We haven't found so much as a seed, but there is a certain

lingering odor in the air. Either it was a processing location or someone had a hell of a party."

Marlene cut in. "Who are 'we?' Did you bring a BIA colleague along?"

"No, a close friend from the RCMP."

Knowing just who Tall Wolf meant, Marlene frowned.

The initials were unfamiliar to Freddie, but as quick as his mind was and given the vast data base of information it had to draw on, he swiftly figured them out. "Royal Canadian Mounted Police?"

"Exactly. In the person of my fiancée, Lieutenant Rebecca Bramley." John asked, "Is that you, Freddie?"

The young billionaire grinned, darkening Marlene's mood further. "Yeah, it's me. Looking forward to meeting you, Mr. Tall Wolf. Lieutenant Bramley, too. Despite the absence of people and drugs, do you think someone was using my land illegally?"

"Sure do. This wasn't a Boy Scout jamboree. There's also another element that Rebecca and I haven't been able to figure out. There seems to be a third party involved, apart from whoever operated the drug processing but possibly connected to it as well."

Marlene asked, "What do you mean, Tall Wolf?"

He told her and Freddie about the bear and the automatic weapon fire.

"I definitely heard a man and a woman speaking Spanish. I learned the language in school, but it was the Castilian variant. You know, like learning the Queen's English at Windsor Castle. My mom knows several dialects but she wouldn't speak any of them at home with me. Still, I heard enough Mexican Spanish in Santa Fe, growing up, to recognize what I heard. My money says the man and woman were both recent border crossers."

"The people who work in the camp," Freddie said. "Dope dealers would recruit from illegal immigrants, wouldn't they?"

Marlene gave the young man a mildly critical look.

Even so, it came as a shock to him, never having seen it before.

"If the workers weren't kidnapped outright, they were certainly coerced," she said.

Hearing that, Freddie had the grace to feel sheepish.

A prodigy or not, he was about to be introduced to a whole new world.

John told Marlene, "I agree, but that raises the question: What were these two doing off on their own? That and being heavily armed."

"Did they kill the animal?" Marlene asked.

"Grazed it, enough to drive it off for the moment, but not sufficiently to keep it from moving like a blue streak. Well, maybe a brown and gray streak, being a grizzly."

"That will make it even more dangerous than normal," Marlene said.

"We're well aware," John replied.

"And you're not distressed, Lieutenant Bramley?" Marlene asked.

"I'll cope," she replied tersely. "You would, wouldn't you?"

"How big was this bear?" Freddie asked.

"Big. Pushing its species limits. Maybe 800 pounds," John said.

"Closer to a thousand, I'd say," Rebecca added, a note of bravado in her voice.

"Wow!" Freddie said, "That is too cool, a creature like that living on my land."

John said, "You can bet there are others, but let's get back to the two-legged predators. Rebecca and I, talking things over, think the people behind this operation, having moved their product and their human capital post haste, will come back soon for the infrastructure they left behind. There aren't enough of us to grab all the bad guys, but we could follow them to their new location and then call in the cavalry."

Freddie laughed. "That's a good one, Indians calling in the cavalry."

Marlene didn't take it as a positive sign, Freddie finding Tall Wolf amusing.

She liked it even less when he added, "I want to be in on this.

I want to help track these people, bring them to justice if they're working people as slaves on my property."

"A fine sentiment," John said.

"A fine sentiment, but what?" Marlene added.

"Well, you would have to act as Mr. Strait Arrow's security, Madam Secretary," John conceded.

"Marlene protect me against bears and drug dealers?" Freddie asked.

His tone said maybe he was reconsidering the notion.

John told him, "Marlene could make the devil drop his pitchfork and run, if she wanted."

There was a moment of silence, then Freddie said, "Yeah, you know —"

"You know, too, Tall Wolf," Marlene said, "and some things you should keep to yourself."

John silently agreed and changed the subject. "Are you two going to see Beebs Bandi before coming up to the mountain?"

"Yes," Freddie said. "I want to meet him."

"Do me a favor then," John told him. "Ask if I can have any stink bombs he has left."

After John ended the call, Rebecca asked, "Is Marlene really as tough as all that? Able to scare the devil?"

"I've told you I think she's more than she appears, right?"

"More than human, yeah, but I've always thought you were exaggerating for effect. Being funny."

"Humor is often the point, but not always. The gunshot that hit Marlene would have killed any normal person, but she was ready to meet the press the next day, in makeup and with her hair styled."

Rebecca gave that a moment's thought. "Should I be afraid of her?"

John shook his head. "She'd only like that, but Marlene knows my mother would take vengeance on her if she came after either of us. Mom really likes you."

"And you've told me your mother is, among other things, a witch."

"Right."

"Is your father anything more than a semi-retired physician?"

"Dad has his scary side, too, but he's kind of private about it."

"How's he feel about me?"

"Thinks of you as a daughter, much beloved."

"Okay, then. So all we have to worry about is the wild life and the drug dealers with automatic weapons."

John sighed and said, "I'd still like to know about that man and woman whose voices we heard. They seem betwixt and between. Maybe not bad guys themselves, but definitely armed and potentially dangerous."

"It's always the wild cards you have to watch out for," Rebecca said.

CHAPTER 23

Gig Harbor — Washington State

Two of the airplanes that had been forced to circle Seattle-Tacoma Airport because Freddie Strait Arrow's 737 went to the head of the line were Mateo Trujillo's Dassault Falcon and an Air Canada Airbus A321 out of Calgary. Forty-five minutes beyond scheduled arrival time passed before both planes arrived at their gates and all the passengers from both flights had disembarked.

An hour and a half went by before Trujillo met with four fashionably bearded men who'd flown down from north of the border. All of the visitors from Calgary had trained with Joint Task Force 2, Canada's elite special operations unit, until they'd all washed out. Not for lack of physical ability or combat prowess but because of conduct contrary to good order and discipline.

More simply put, they had proved adept at killing but lacked respect for the chain of command. They'd run afoul of the rules and regs to the point where each of them had been locked up in Club Ed, the Canadian Forces Service Prison and Detention Barracks in Edmonton. Each had served a sentence of one day short of two years, the point at which they would have had to be transferred to the civilian prison system. Instead, they were released from confinement and military service.

They were warned before they departed confinement that they would be back behind bars quickly if they ever talked in public about their training or the types of missions they would have participated in had they not proven to be such incorrigible pricks.

Mateo Trujillo, with his CIA connections, knew all about those missions and these four men as well. Their names were Able, Baker, Charlie and Dog. Not really. But that's how they referred to themselves when working. Old school phonetic military alphabet. It also delineated their pecking order. Along with other non-governmental talent scouts to whom military etiquette was secondary to a confirmed kill, Mateo had made contact with the four men shortly after they'd been cashiered. He'd used their services previously and found them satisfactory.

As luck would have it, their schedule was open when he called them en route to Seattle. They were able to head out at a moment's notice, once Mateo agreed to meet their fee. He thought it spoke well of the mercenaries' preparedness that they could be ready on short notice … that or they hadn't been hired for a while and were getting desperate for work.

Mateo met the mercenaries in Gig Harbor, a cozy suburban hamlet near Tacoma where a dispute over the high school reading list was considered high drama. No one at the brew-pub where they gathered at a corner table ever would have suspected that the actual shedding of blood was being planned in their midst. To Mateo's eye, his hired guns were clear-eyed, neatly dressed and well behaved. Business men in their casual clothes, getting an early start on a Saturday evening of good-natured camaraderie.

The capitalist imperative of making money had succeeded in teaching the men good manners and civil behavior where the military had failed. The difference in incentive was easy to measure. Thousands of dollars a dollar a day versus the same amount per month.

Mateo was happy to see none of the men seemed at all desperate.

He'd just caught them at the right time.

After their drinks and meal orders had been served and the waiter had departed, Mateo said, in a voice lower than the babble of neighboring conversations, "My hope is we will have an easy time with this chore. All we need to do is make sure that a business that is relocating from Point A to Point B continues to operate in an equally productive fashion."

Able spoke for all the mercenaries in every business occasion short of life-or-death necessity. "What might prevent that from happening?"

Mateo enumerated four possibilities, extending a finger for each one.

"Management might need to be thinned by half; the workers might need to be reminded of their obligations; the security people will need to be vetted for wavering allegiance and ... let's just say we'll have to check for industrial saboteurs."

Baker caught Able's eye and sent a silent message.

Able told Mateo, "My friend wants to know if you mean a cyber attack?"

Mateo shook his head. "Not at all. This is strictly within your area of expertise."

All four mercenaries understood the briefing: They'd have to scare some people, maybe pop a few, and hunt down someone else, his fate also likely being terminal. In other words, no big deal. Easy money.

"You've made the travel arrangements?" Able asked Mateo.

"Yes." Meaning he'd provide their wheels and knew where to go. "You'll bring all your equipment?" Meaning weapons, ammunition, body armor and survival gear.

Able nodded. "We'll do our shopping right after we eat."

Putting a military level assault on a credit card was easier in the U.S. than anywhere else in the world.

Mateo was pleased, sure they would succeed. He would complete the last job he'd ever do for Fausto Zara and neither the cartel boss nor anyone else would suspect him of the treachery he had in mind. And if anything went wrong ...

Well, assuming that no one at the table in the brew-pub went toes up, the Canadians could race across their border and had wilderness to hide in that extended into the Arctic, and the survival skills to make do in such primal conditions. As for him, he could run south of the Mexican border as far as Tierra del Fuego, if need be.

Mateo wouldn't live off the land but would pay off anyone necessary to survive.

Between them, they could leave the length of two continents for any pursuers to search.

He liked his chances. Everyone at the table was feeling good when the waiter returned.

"Anybody in the mood for dessert?" the waiter asked.

CHAPTER 24

Cascade Mountains — Washington State

Julián thought his idiot cousin, Basilio, would never get within a mile of killing Freddie Strait Arrow, and if he tried he would surely be gunned down by the billionaire's security people. Julián had done a research paper on the ten richest people in the United States to see how they protected themselves. The original intent of the paper was to reveal the strategies they used to safeguard their fortunes. How they hedged their financial bets, that was.

His professor liked the idea but told Julián to broaden his focus and to see how the truly wealthy also insulated their holdings politically. What was the extent of their influence on the passage of advantageous laws and the formulation of favorable federal rules that might add to their wealth? Discover the extent to which these activities might be considered legitimate and what strategies were clearly, if covertly, corrupt.

Julián had liked that angle and ran with it. Getting inside information on those titans was not easy, of course, but Julián knew people who knew people. The information he included in his paper made his professor's jaw drop.

"This is astounding," the prof said. "These people not only influence the government, they *own* parts of it in everything but name. But you didn't name your sources for this information."

"They'd kill me if I did," Julián said. "I'm not kidding about that. I just wanted you to see what I found out. I'm going to omit that section from the final draft I submit to you."

The professor had dealt with all sorts of student subterfuge when it came to schemes for grade boosting, but that wasn't the feeling he got from this young man. Julián was a Mexican national. Seemed well heeled, too. Hadn't asked the university for a penny in financial add. He might have personal experience in what the wealthy in his own country did to protect themselves.

If that was the case, it wouldn't be such a big jump to find out how others did it. The professor said, "Well, thank you for this personal glimpse of how these things work, Julián. Maybe someday you'll be able to publicly source your material. You'd have the foundation for a best-selling book here."

Julián edited his paper and still got an A. He thought he'd scared his professor a little bit.

Would have terrified him if he'd known Fausto Zara's people had provided the information. It was no big deal to them. Julián was a member of the family and he'd paid them for what he wanted. If what he did compromised the lofty perches of a bunch of fat *yanquis,* well, that would be good for a laugh.

Zara's *compadres* were able to provide the information in the first place because the filthy rich around the world, regardless of where they lived or how they came by their money, used the same security strategists: former military, intelligence officers and federal police. Men with expertise in violence who wanted to make some money of their own.

The security men knew about the bankers, lawyers and influence peddlers who sustained and enlarged the holdings of their patrons. They were all leeches bleeding the common man, who rarely if ever realized he was being sucked dry. They kept that sad creature anesthetized with sports, gambling, sex, video violence, alcohol and, of course, drugs.

Writing that paper had changed Julián's life. He had thought of going into investment banking, but even those *cabrónes* didn't make their money as quickly as someone who could prove himself valuable to Fausto Zara. Julián became someone who had developed a new channel for making *El Jefe* large sums of money. Better yet, he'd done so in the face of the new and daunting challenge of competing with legalized marijuana.

The reward for his ingenuity and two years of hard work was $20 million in his Cayman Islands bank account and the growing esteem of the most powerful drug boss in the world. His future should have been ever more golden, and it looked to be …until that pendejo with his camera showed up out of nowhere.

In that moment, Julián experienced an epiphany: He realized his downfall hadn't been a random event. The photographer hadn't simply wandered into Julián's life. Freddie Strait Arrow had *sent* him. For what purpose, he didn't know, but —

He was snapped out of his reverie when Basilio shook his shoulder.

"Have you gone deaf, Julián? I'm trying to talk to you."

Julián slapped Basilio's hand away and got to his feet. "What do you want? There had better not be any trouble."

Basilio shook his head. "Not with the *campesinos*."

"Then what?"

"It's me. I … I forgot something. Back at the old camp."

"Ay, mierda. You can fetch it tomorrow. You'll take the others to bring back our tents and other necessities."

"Yes, yes, I can do that. But I would like to go tonight. What I forgot is important to me."

Julián knew his cousin liked to carry an absurd amount of money around with him. He stuffed his wallet fat with cash. Such a stupid thing to do. Basilio had $2 million in his own Cayman account. But he liked flashing gringo dollars. It made him feel important. Never mind that so much currency would be a lure and a windfall for street thugs. It would also make any cop who stopped him suspicious. How had this *cabron* come by so much money?

For all his love of tangible buying power, though, Julián felt it was more than money that motivated his cousin. Made him want to set off through the wilderness in the gathering darkness.

"Is it that picture of you and those four *putas* you can't do without?" he asked.

Basilio's jaw dropped in surprise. "You know about that?"

Julián rolled his eyes. "I know you jerk off *el pene* every night. I can't help but hear you. I saw the photo sticking out of your wallet one day, so I looked."

Basilio's face turned red with indignation — and then he relaxed. Which was all the giveaway Julián needed. "There's something else."

Basilio shook his head. "No, no. Nothing else."

"Yes, there is." The answer came to him intuitively. "Jesus, did you manage to get a picture of Valeria Batista?"

Knowing there was no point in trying to deceive his damnably smart cousin, Basilio confessed. "Only with her clothes on. Just her face, really. But I'd trade the other four for her."

Expecting a rebuke, Basilio was pleasantly surprised when his cousin laid a compassionate hand on his shoulder and said, "If the picture means that much to you, if Señora Batista has such a hold on your heart, go get the picture. This moment, if that's what you want."

Basilio embraced Julián. "You will be the best man at my wedding someday."

"Of course."

"Is there anything else I should bring back or just wait for the others and then bring everything?"

"Use your best judgment," Julián said.

Basilio kissed his cousin's cheek and was off.

Julián watched until Basilio was out of sight. He'd known from the beginning that Basilio was on hand not just to keep the *campesinos* and the guards in line. If Fausto Zara ever decided Julián had outlived his usefulness, he would need someone nearby to kill him.

Basilio.

That was just good management. Zara should have known Julián would see that.

So in the face of the present potential calamity it was only wise for Julián to allow Basilio to head off into the forest in the dark where he might fall and break his neck, encounter a wild animal that might devour him or come face to face with Ernesto Batista, who had to be far more resourceful than he appeared, and would defend his wife to the death.

Basilio's death. *Adios,* cousin.

CHAPTER 25

Cascade Mountains — Washington State

Rebecca was still worried about the bear, but she sucked it up and told John she'd be alright occupying an ambush site by herself. "I can do it."

She kept her bow and the MK14 sniper rifle. She also accepted a spare Glock G43 compact semi-auto sidearm the John said he'd forgotten he had brought along.

"Forgotten, hah," Rebecca said.

"If you wind up shooting someone with it, you'll have to give me credit," he told her. "Special Agent Mulgrew slipped it to me on the way out the FBI's door."

"Nice guy. If I use it to bag the bear, though, credit for that is all mine."

John kept the MP5 submachine gun and took up his position. They were hiding in darkened tents at the base points of a right triangle. The apex was the tent with the two bunks and the wallet with the money and the Polaroids. They'd left that tent as they'd found it with the exception of turning on a battery-powered lantern.

In the darkness of the mountain night, a yellow magnet of light flowed from the open flap of the tent, as welcoming as a lover's embrace. Or the dead giveaway of a trap, if you had the least bit of a suspicious nature. John and Rebecca had made allowances for the fact that not all of the bad guys might be gullible.

They'd also agreed on the likelihood that some of the people who'd abandoned the marijuana processing camp would be back soon. They'd made off with all of the dope and the workers, but they'd left behind a wealth of infrastructure: tents, bedding, cooking equipment and all the paraphernalia needed to grow and process cannabis on a commercial scale.

They'd found barrels of natural soil nutrients, biopesticides with a low adverse soil impact, and a large stove-like device with a huge chimney-form rising out of it.

"What the heck is that?" Rebecca had asked.

John looked at a label affixed to the metal beast. "A drying and curing machine."

"Damn, this making dope stuff is getting to be big business, if someone's designing that kind of equipment for it. But where the heck do you plug that thing in?"

John looked behind the device. "Portable generator. Looks like solar powered."

"So no bad chemicals in the fertilizer and pesticides, and no gas fumes expended in the processing. The grass grown here was environmentally green."

"Produces a lot of money, too, so that's another kind of green. And making electricity from sunlight is silent, so no racket from a fuel-powered generator either. This is one slick set-up."

"Somebody's going to come back soon," Rebecca said, "if only to scavenge."

John nodded. "I can't think of a better place to spend a night in the woods, and if we can nab a bad guy or two in the process so much the better."

"You think they've got some organic bear repellent here?" she asked.

"Maybe they just sacrificed malcontents to the predators. Tied the whiners to a stake to keep everyone else in line."

Rebecca winced. "Human sacrifice? Is this your Aztec side finally coming out?"

"Too *outré?*" John asked. French for outlandish.

"*Encore plus.*" More than. Canada being a bilingual country,

Rebecca could more than hold her own in French.

"*Désolé.*" Sorry.

They'd let it go at that and set up their ambush points.

Two hours later, as it was getting hard for John and Rebecca to fight off fatigue, a woman crept into camp, stepping into the cone of light coming from the target tent. Looking around, she revealed herself to be young and pretty. She stepped into the tent.

By John's silent count it took ten seconds before she cried out, "*¡Dios santo!*" Dear God!

John, playing home-country advantage, had told Rebecca he'd make the first move. She would act only if it looked like he'd stepped in the poop and might get buried in it. Now, he hoped she'd follow the plan.

The woman continued to cry out, "*Ay, dios!*"

Her voice tread a fine line between agony and ecstasy.

John was sure that someone waiting just out of sight was with the woman, but it was only when she stopped addressing the Almighty and called out, "*¡Ernesto, venga aquí!*" that a man carrying a rifle finally appeared. He ducked into the tent.

But he didn't exclaim at whatever had excited his companion.

And she fell silent, too.

John waited, exercising a hunter's patience, hoping Rebecca would, too.

She did and their forbearance was rewarded.

A second man, holding a handgun, slipped out of the darkness and dashed into the tent.

Within the space of a heartbeat, a gun was fired.

CHAPTER 26

Tesla — Washington State

Marlene Flower Moon, the Acting Secretary of the Interior and John Tall Wolf's nominal boss, sat bolt upright in bed with the feral alertness of an animal sensing that its den had been invaded. Something, somewhere was threatening Marlene's interests. A low snarl boiled out of her throat. Not loud enough to wake Freddie Strait Arrow sleeping at her side. She'd drained him of all the energy he'd possessed beyond what was necessary to keep his heart beating.

The two of them occupied the master bedroom of the finest house in the hamlet. Beebs Bandi slept downstairs in a small room off the kitchen. Marlene's ears seemed to grow points as she listened for any sound elsewhere in the house. Hearing nothing, she sniffed the air. Her nose told her the photographer was right where he should be: asleep in his bed.

For a second, it amused her that Bandi could sleep so peacefully.

A young man with a clear conscience. Just like the one sleeping next to her. What was the world coming to? Where were all the rascals and troublemakers? Well, no problem, she'd been known to lead many a Boy Scout astray.

Not that she'd succeeded in corrupting Tall Wolf, after many years of trying. With Freddie well in hand, she might have lost interest in Tall Wolf, but try as she might, she couldn't let him go. The more he resisted her, the more she wanted him to bend to her will. Their fates were locked together.

Tall Wolf had joked with her that when she finally got to devour him she might not like the way he tasted. He could well be right about that. It wouldn't matter though. The taste of him could be as bitter as the memory of a lost love but she'd still take satisfaction in every bite.

Now, though, she sensed Tall Wolf was in danger.

The threat could be found in the nearby mountain forest. She opened a window to the chill night air and lifted her nose high. There were other people near Tall Wolf, but they weren't the danger. Tall Wolf could handle them. He always did. No, this peril belonged to …

The points on Marlene's ears sharpened and grew taller. She could hear the beat of a mighty heart now and recognized the rage within its thumping percussion. Brother Bear. He was furious and determined to have his vengeance. He was watching from the woods, biding his time, waiting for the perfect moment to attack.

But what had Tall Wolf done to Brother Bear?

Marlene couldn't imagine Tall Wolf indulging in any casual cruelty to what he probably regarded as an animal. He certainly wouldn't partake in anything so vile as trophy hunting. Tall Wolf's mother knew that the spirits of wild creatures were powerful. She would have taught him better than to take any life that didn't threaten his own.

Had Brother Bear been the transgressor? Had he tried to make a meal of Tall Wolf? That possibility raised Marlene's ire. Tall Wolf's fate belonged to her. No other creature great or small would take him from her.

She'd have to intervene. Have a long talk with Brother Bear. A mirthless smile came to Marlene's lips. When the time came for her to testify before Congress at her confirmation hearing to be Secretary of the Interior, how would her inquisitors react if she let them see exactly how qualified she was for the job?

The thought of the throng running from the hearing room drew a small laugh from her.

A cold breeze wafted her way and now she had a better idea of who Tall Wolf's human company out there in the forest was. His woman, Bramley, was with him. So was another female and two men, one of them bleeding. The scent of blood sent a thrill racing through her.

While lost in that primal rush, Freddie managed to surprise Marlene.

Speaking in a sleepy voice, he said, "Hey, come back to bed, will you? And close the window. I'm freezing."

Marlene lowered the window, letting her everyday appearance reassert itself before Freddie could notice how she had changed.

Wouldn't do to have him say, "My, what big teeth you have, Grandma."

She slipped into bed beside him, turning up her body heat as she embraced him.

"Go back to sleep," Marlene whispered. "We have to get up early."

CHAPTER 27

Cascade Mountains — Washington State

As John entered the tent, the round-faced man with the assault rifle in his hands was on his feet; the guy who'd brought a handgun to a rifle fight was flat on his back, out cold and bleeding from his right shoulder. The fact that his blood still flowed told John that the guy's heart was still pumping. John wasn't worried about that. He had his MP5 pointing at the guy who had his weapon, an M16 knockoff, trained on him.

Rebecca had her little Glock pointed at the other woman in the tent, who appeared to be unarmed at the moment, but might have something up her sleeve. You never knew.

Before anyone could suffer the proverbial itchy trigger finger, John asked the man, "*¿Habla inglés, señor?*"

"*Sí*, yes, I do."

John said, "I am a federal officer. Do you understand?"

"FBI?"

"Bureau of Indian Affairs."

The man frowned. "This is Indian land?"

"It's private property owned by a Native American."

A smile of genuine amusement lit the man's face. "Even *los indios* are rich in *El Norte?*"

John smiled back. "Some. This one in particular."

"What about you?"

"I make do with my salary."

By now, John had seen the man's casual comfort with his weapon. He was relaxed but ready to fire the moment he saw hostile intent enter John's eyes. He'd been well trained.

"You are a soldier, *señor?*"

A flicker of surprise crossed the man's face. "Not many see that. I was *un marino.*"

"A marine. So you not only know how to use your weapon, you also know duty and discipline — and honor." John took things a step farther and played a hunch. "That was why you spared the life of the boy with the camera."

The Mexican woman reacted with a comical look of surprise. She turned to the man with the assault rifle and said, "*¿Cómo sabía eso?*"

Asking how John knew that. About Ernesto sparing the boy.

In the tension of the moment, she'd forgotten John had spoken Spanish.

To Rebecca's credit, she remained stoic, silent and ready, though she hadn't understood what the Mexican woman had said.

"*Señor,*" the man said to John. "I am curious also how you knew this."

"I met the young man with the camera. He told me he didn't know how you missed him. I know. You didn't kill him because that was not your intention. You are not a man who kills without a good reason."

John slowly lowered the MP5 and extended his hand. "I'm John Tall Wolf."

Still cautious, the man with the assault rifle asked, "Do you know who that *cabrón* is?"

He pointed to the bleeding figure on the ground. John saw the flow of blood had stopped. Either clotting was taking place or the guy's heart had quit. John felt no great concern. Chances were humanity wouldn't weep at his passing.

"I think he's the man whose wallet your lady friend found. He probably came back for it."

The billfold was now on top of the pillow not beneath it.

"I did not take any money," she said.

John shrugged. "I'm not concerned about that. Besides, he took a photograph of you. My impression was he caught you unaware."

The man and woman looked at each other.

John said, "It's in the wallet."

She opened the wallet, found the Polaroids and took them out. Made a disgusted sound and said, "*Puerco*," pig, when she saw the first one. The quartet of nudies. She tossed it on the bed and was even more disturbed when she saw the next shot.

Without a word, she passed it to the man with the rifle, who lowered his weapon and clicked on the safety. He studied the picture, smiled and shook his head. "*Estás siempre fotogénica.*"

Photogenic as always.

John whispered a translation to Rebecca.

The man extended his hand to John. "*Ernesto Batista y mi esposa, Valeria.*"

John introduced Rebecca, "My fiancée, Lieutenant Rebecca Bramley of the Royal Canadian Mounted Police."

The Mexican couple was surprised to learn of Rebecca's nationality and police affiliation, but kept any questions they may have had to themselves. Valeria, though, seemed to find the idea of a female Mountie interesting.

In the face of social courtesies, Rebecca pocketed her Glock and shook the Batistas' hands. The expression on Ernesto's face clearly said he wanted to know what the Mounties' interest was and to make sure he hadn't traveled farther north than he'd ever thought. But his wife beat him to the verbal punch.

She told John, "*Señor*, my husband and I have worked very hard. May we please keep the money I found?"

"*No, es mio.*" It's mine.

Everyone turned to look. The guy who'd been shot was staging a comeback, propping himself up on his good arm and asserting a claim to the money. "*Es mio.*"

Valeria kicked him in the thigh, drawing a howl. She flicked the picture of the uninhibited ladies at him. He actually managed to snag it out of the air and stuffed it in a pocket.

Ernesto asked John, "May I kill this man?"

"What's his name?"

"Basilio Nuñez."

John looked at the now fearful figure on the ground. *"¿Basilio, me puede dar una razón para que usted vive?"* Can you give me a reason to let you live?

Basilio replied in rapid-fire Spanish until he ran out of breath. Then he clasped his hands in a prayerful manner and gave John a beseeching look.

"Is that right?" John asked the Batistas.

With a look of both disgust and regret, Ernesto nodded. *"Sí."*

Valeria gave Basilio another kick and bobbed her head in agreement.

John translated for Rebecca. "The guy who got shot claims he's a little turd but he can give us a lot of the big shits."

Rebecca said, "Give you, *kemosabe*. I'm just a visiting Canadienne."

Valeria, with Nuñez's wallet in hand, thought the moment right to renew her plea. "The money, *señor?*"

John said, "It has to be the proceeds of a criminal enterprise, so you really don't want it."

"I do," Valeria insisted.

John looked at Ernesto. He had an M16 knockoff resting upright against his right leg, but he wasn't about to argue with his unarmed wife. Smart man.

"Señora," John said, "I know of the man who owns all this land. He is a very rich Indian. I'm sure he will reward you for helping to capture this man who was using his land illegally. I will ask him to match the money in that wallet dollar for dollar — and the money he gives you won't come with any bad luck attached. I mean, look at what happened to Mr. Nuñez when he came back for it."

Valeria needed only a second to consider those words.

She dropped the wallet and the money, but kept the Polaroid bearing her likeness.

John couldn't begrudge her that.

CHAPTER 28

Sunday, October 18, 2015
Cascade Mountains — Washington State

In the first light of day, Beebs Bandi snapped a photograph from his perch on the ridge. He had the huge SUV on the road below, a black Lincoln Navigator, smack dab in his telephoto lens. The vehicle looked ominous in its own right, but what really scared Beebs was the guy in the front passenger seat. He took sitting shotgun very seriously.

He didn't have a pump-action Remington in hand; he held what looked like an assault rifle. Having recent experience as the target of such a weapon, it sent a chill through Beebs. The Navigator's windshield was clean as a whistle and had no sun reflecting off the glass so Beebs tripped the shutter on his camera and got a good picture of the man and his weapon. In Texas, a guy riding in a $60,000 truck with an assault weapon in hand might only be making a statement, fashion or political.

In Washington State, Beebs felt sure he saw bad news coming down the road. He knew he had to get back to Tesla to let Freddie and that hot Indian babe, Marlene, know. The Navigator had to take the winding mountain road slow. Beebs had a shorter, more direct line back to town on foot. If he didn't break his neck jumping from ledge to ledge, he thought he could get there in time to sound the alarm.

Tesla, Washington State

Marlene was awake and stood naked at the bedroom window once more, looking down at the only road in Tesla. Cute place, she thought. With the advent of indoor plumbing and central heating, there was no reason someone couldn't spend the winter there. All you'd need was enough food and drink in the freezer and pantry. Fuel and solar to generate electricity. If you got snowed in, so what? Spring always came.

It struck her as a fine place for someone who needed to hide out.

When you owned the whole place, you could set up your own movie theater in one of the buildings. Maybe build an skating rink. Go snowmobiling through the forest. Sit in an outdoor hot-tub looking up at the frozen stars. Enjoy just about any kind of amenity you wanted. Set aside one of the dwellings for the help. They could cook and clean, clear snow from sidewalks and the road.

And if you didn't need to hide out, you could rent the place to someone who did.

Marlene believed in making the most of her resources.

She'd talk to Freddie about the idea when the time was right.

All of Marlene's scheming was put on hold the moment she saw Beebs sprinting down the road as if the hour of his death would arrive any second. Was Brother Bear hot on his heels, she wondered. She'd thought she sensed the animal lurking nearby last night. But seconds passed and no fur-bearing predator appeared hot on Beebs' heels. Still, the young man, clasping his camera to his side, sped onward.

He had to be heading for Freddie's house.

Marlene threw on a robe and, moving faster than Beebs could ever hope to, met him at the front door.

"What's wrong?" she asked.

Beebs needed a moment to catch his breath. When Marlene lost patience with his recovery time, she grabbed his shoulders. "What is it?"

"SUV coming," he gasped. "Guy in front seat has assault rifle." He stopped to think for a moment, regaining a greater capacity to speak. "It's a damn big truck, a black Navigator. Might be more than just two guys. What the hell do they want?"

Marlene made the immediate assumption that the armed men were coming to protect their marijuana, maybe to *persuade* the landowner that he was going to let the operation continue and keep his mouth shut about it, if he wanted to go on living. On the other hand, they might just intend to kill Freddie and let his death be a warning to anyone else whose land they were appropriating.

Or they might simply be kidnappers. Out to demand millions for Freddie's freedom.

That was a far more common crime in Mexico than in the U.S., but maybe kidnapping was something else that was now crossing the border.

Whatever the case, Marlene wasn't going to let any harm befall Freddie nor was she going to permit anyone else to direct the choices he made. She'd remove Freddie from harm's way ... and she'd give these interlopers a warning of her own. Something they couldn't ignore.

She squeezed Beebs' shoulders harder. "How soon will they be here?"

"Five minutes, maybe." Scared as he was of the guys in the truck, and now Marlene, too, Beebs couldn't help but wish he could raise his camera and take a photo of Marlene's face. Her eyes, they were like something you'd see in a wild animal ... and her teeth, Jesus, they were fangs.

"I'll take Mr. Strait Arrow into the woods," she told Beebs. "You will stay in town. You will hide. You will find a way to contact me and let me know what you see. Do you understand?"

A part of Beebs' mind wanted to shout: *Are you freaking crazy?*

Only, without a hint of why it was happening, he was getting hard.

The woman simply had her hands on his shoulders, but she was filling him with a sexual thrill unlike anything he'd ever experienced.

Not only was he getting excited, he also felt stronger than ever before. Heroic, even. He wanted to rush out and meet that Navigator head on, smash it, beat anyone inside it into a pulp. Grind their bones to dust under his heels.

He would have tried to do just that, only Marlene told him, "Run, hide, watch, report."

Coming from her, that worked for Beebs, too.

He ran through the house and out the back door.

Within two minutes, Marlene and Freddie had also left Tesla.

Mateo Trujillo's first thought upon seeing Tesla through the windshield of the Navigator was: *This'd be a cool place to hide out.* Mountains always made the best refuges. He knew there were those who preferred jungles or remote islands, but jungles were breeding grounds for gruesome diseases and the humidity alone was enough to make you wish you were dead. An island, if it had its own freshwater supply, might be bearable for a while, but you'd have to import all your other needs, and that would be a giveaway to anyone hunting you.

The only problem he saw with Tesla was its road; the pavement didn't dead-end at the town. It continued on to somewhere else. That meant drive-through traffic. No hideout of his could have that. You'd never be able to tell if your enemies had found you or innocent passersby were just rubbernecking as they went past.

But a place similar to this one with a sign, maybe two miles outside its limits, saying "Road Ends," would be perfect. Put up a private property sign a mile out with a couple of armed men to enforce your privacy and no one would ever know you were there. Well, they could snoop on you with aircraft or drones, but you could harass aircraft or shoot down drones with your own UAVs.

Mateo wasn't just daydreaming. His imminent betrayal of Fausto Zara would likely result in either *el jefe's* death or his lifelong incarceration in an American super-max prison. That wouldn't mean Mateo was safe, though. Even the boss's enemies would want to kill Mateo, just to make an example of him. Show their men what happened to traitors.

Zara's own men, the ones who were loyal and aspired to rebuild *el jefe's* empire would also be looking for him. Their idea of vengeance would be especially bloodthirsty. No simple bullet to the head for him. His death at their hands would be a drawn-out exercise in sadism, each moment more excruciating than the preceding one.

His only hope was to evade the vengeful long enough that imprisonment or the need to run from their own pursuers would make them focus on more important matters. That and the legalization of drugs in *El Norte* cutting their revenue to the vanishing point.

Marijuana was already on its way to widespread acceptance.

Cocaine would be next.

Hard drugs would be dispensed in medical settings, just like in Portugal.

After that, drug cartels would become as obsolete as oil cartels once renewable energy technology made its inevitable breakthroughs. The bosses south of the Rio Grande could try to muscle their way into local production and distribution within *los estados unidos* — that's what Julián Fortuna was attempting in the nearby forest, with spotty results — but once the big *yanqui* corporations got involved in selling recreational drugs, illegal competition from any quarter would be crushed.

Mateo, with his access to intelligence reports and his position within Fausto Zara's organization, had no trouble seeing all these things coming. He'd been planning his exit — his escape — for the last five years. What he hadn't anticipated, but should have, he supposed, was the idea that Zara and the other bosses, no doubt, would attempt military insurrection. Take over the government in Mexico and rule the country openly, not just exert influence from the shadows.

If Zara was able to get his hands on a squadron of A-10s and find the pilots to fly them, the bloodshed would be horrific and the foundation of Mexico's society would be destroyed. The Americans would never stand for the presence of an openly autocratic, violent and unpredictable government on their southern border. For all they knew, Mexico might try to reclaim all of the southwestern United States.

Reconquista? Bullshit.

Mexico would be crushed and Washington would exert direct rule all the way down to the Panama Canal, and God help South America if it got testy about things. Mateo Trujillo wanted none of that to happen. So he would betray Fausto Zara, put an end to his *coup d'état* madness, and retire with a great deal of money to some beautiful mountain setting like this one.

But first he had to put an end to Julián Fortuna's foolish experiment.

Kill whoever needed killing, pick up the few million dollars in bribe money Julián had lying around, and make contact with his friends in the CIA.

Freddie Strait Arrow's head was still spinning as he sat leaning against a tree just outside of Tesla. It seemed like only seconds ago he'd been tucked in bed having the most wonderful of dreams. Unlike most people, Freddie almost always dreamed in black and white. That was fine by him because he didn't dream of old girlfriends — he didn't have any — or embarrassing schoolroom scenes where he showed up not wearing pants or having left the assigned work undone — neither of those things had ever happened.

No, Freddie's dreams, especially the best ones, were always the same. He stood at a board, an old fashioned blackboard, with a stick of white chalk in hand. At a speed he could never match while conscious, he would whip out the most amazing formulas expressing mathematical relationships that nobody had ever thought of much less seen before. Diagrams of molecules arranged to form new compounds and undreamed of materials also appeared on the board as if produced by a magic wand.

The best thing about this subconscious conjuring was Freddie could remember every detail perfectly when he awoke. Put it all down on paper. Add it to a computer, one not linked to any external network. A machine password protected by a 52-symbol sequence that a super-computer couldn't crack, but Freddie could remember off the top of his head.

Because he never forgot anything.

Until that morning, anyway. Freddie had forgotten almost everything about the dream he was having when Marlene had yanked him out of bed. He hadn't been ready to wake up. No, no, no. He could still feel the pain of his newest and best insight into the workings of the universe slip away from him. He felt as if he'd had part of his mind severed from his body.

He wanted to scream in agony, but Marlene overrode the impulse with the scariest look he'd ever seen from anyone or anything.

"Men are coming," she said. "They might mean to kill or kidnap you."

Freddie was still trying to register the shock of that notion when Marlene pulled him from bed as if his body was made of balsa. His clothes appeared on his body as magically as his equations did on the blackboard. Then he was moving as if being swept along by his own personal windstorm. Not quite a tornado, but something approaching that sensation.

Within the space of what seemed to be a heartbeat, he was rushed out of the house, the world a blur around him. Moments later, he was in the woods, a quarter-mile away by his usually accurate sense of distance. Only he didn't know which of his faculties he could trust anymore, what with his memory of the breakthrough concept he'd been putting on his blackboard completely gone.

He'd never had a personal failure like that before ... but he'd never been yanked out of bed so urgently either. It wasn't unreasonable to think the rude interruption of his subconscious mind had proved his undoing. Only Marlene had said she was saving his life or at least his freedom.

He had to wonder about that. He'd been warned by his parents that his sudden accumulation of great wealth would make him a target for both con artists and gangsters. Some of whom might well be girls or women. He hadn't worried about the grifters; he doubted there was anyone in the world who could out-think him. As for the criminals with guns, well, they were the stuff of TV, movies and video games weren't they?

Maybe not. After all, he'd never have suspected anyone like Marlene existed. She'd simply walked right up to him and made her pitch. He'd found it compelling, slept with her and now he had to admit he found her company, especially in bed, all but addictive.

Then there were the things she could do that seemed supernatural.

Maybe she'd figured out formulas even he couldn't imagine.

That was another part of her appeal for him.

Marlene was the only person he'd ever dreamed of in color.

Vivid colors.

For all that, he wasn't sure he'd trade what she'd brought into his life for what he might lose. He'd be heartbroken if he couldn't recover the breakthrough he'd experienced that morning. Problem was, he'd never had a recurring dream, had never needed one.

Then, Jesus, an even scarier thought popped into his head: What if he'd lost his *blackboard* permanently? Would never have *any* more breakthrough concepts.

That horrifying idea might have made Freddie weep.

Only a more immediate and mortal terror appeared.

Looking up, Freddie saw an enormous brown bear eyeing him from thirty feet away.

The beast pulled back it lips, revealing great daggers of teeth and began to growl.

And took its first step toward Freddie.

Mateo and the four Canadian mercenaries got out of the Navigator in front of the biggest house in Tesla. The assault rifle each of them carried seemed harshly at odds with the row of gingerbread Victorian homes and shops. Barbarians were crashing the tea party.

The niceties would not be observed.

Able posted Charlie to watch the road through town, keep any traffic from stopping.

"Rules of engagement?" Charlie asked.

"Yell, first. Brandish your weapon, second. Fire a round in the air, third."

The fourth step wasn't necessary to verbalize.

"If a cop stops?" Charlie asked.

"Smoke him." Turning to Mateo, he added. "Killing a cop or two will cost you extra."

Mateo said, "Just don't let them call for help. I'm not paying for a war."

Able looked at Charlie. "Understood?"

Charlie smiled and nodded. He was good with his parameters.

Able told Dog, "Check the rear entrances of all these structures. We don't want anyone slipping out the back door or firing on us from an outhouse."

"What if I see a lady hanging clothes out to dry?"

"Leave the clothes, corral the lady. Any civilians you find, round them up."

"And then?" Dog asked.

Able turned back to Mateo. "Your call, life or death. Each fatality over the first ten will cost extra. Double for women and kids."

Sarcasm in his voice, Mateo said, "You'll throw in pets for free?"

Able laughed. "Cats, sure. Guard dogs, too. Anything else we can negotiate."

Mateo said, "In the interests of decency and sound budgeting, don't kill anyone who isn't an immediate threat to your lives or mine."

He also didn't want to stick the CIA with too big a mess to clean up.

Able looked at his men. If there were going to be witnesses left behind, he and his men couldn't let their faces be seen. They pulled the stocking caps on their heads down over their faces. There were openings for their eyes, noses and mouths. Now, they looked like bank-robbers or terrorists. All to the good for purposes of intimidation.

You hid your face, you dehumanized yourself.

You became a monster capable of inflicting any kind of brutality.

Only problem was, Able had the feeling this move, hiding their features, should have been discussed before they had exited the Navigator. If Able got the feeling somebody might have gotten a look at him and his men before they pulled their caps down, he was going to kill them.

He could argue money for the extra kills with the greaser afterward.

Able was sure Mateo would see things his way.

Charlie stayed out front; Dog ran to the back of the big house they would enter first. Baker kicked in the front door, and Able ran inside, his weapon at the ready. Mateo lingered behind on the front porch. No sense in risking his life, he thought, when he was paying someone else to do his dirty work.

Beebs Bandi, ever the ace photographer, had set himself up in an attic of a house down the street at a curve in the road with an angle on just about every other structure in town. He'd seen the Navigator arrive. Saw the men exit the SUV. Could have killed them all, if he'd had the right firearm and disposition.

Massacres weren't his thing, though.

Still, he did nail all five of them with his telephoto lens.

Got sharp, clean shots of each man's face before they pulled down their masks. Photographed the truck, too. Made sure he framed the numbers on the license plate so all of them were in frame. Even the date on the tiny registration sticker was legible.

For the first time since he'd climbed the tree to shoot the young movie stars making love, Beebs felt a sense of redemption. He was going to use his gift for photography to put some bad guys behind bars, and the bastards wouldn't know until it was too late that Bruno

"Beebs" Bandi had brought them to justice.

His sense of confidence flagged when the bad guys started making their moves. Yeah, one of them stayed out on the road, but another ran off behind the house where he, Freddie and Marlene had stayed last night. Then three more of them broke into Freddie's house.

Jesus, what if Freddie and Marlene hadn't gotten out yet?

Freddie had still been in bed a few minutes ago and —

Beebs heard the loudest, most awful scream of his life.

He was sure someone had just died.

Able was the first man through Freddie's door. He was the team leader because he was the best of the bunch. Top marksman, top edged-weapon fighter, top at hand-to-hand combat. He saw the danger while the other guys were still looking for the threat. He reacted faster. He exploited vulnerabilities while the others searched for a point of attack.

Baker, Charlie and Dog followed Able willingly because they knew their chances of staying alive and unhurt were far better with him at the point of the spear.

None of that mattered once the team leader crossed the threshold of Freddie Strait Arrow's house and the monster leapt out of the shadows. Able turned his head in time to see a pair of fiery eyes and an enormous mouthful of teeth flying at him. He didn't have a chance to do anything but scream. Baker, seeing the mangled, fallen Able, couldn't help but recoil.

Able felt, ever so briefly, the agony of his throat being pierced and his cervical spine being crushed. His training never had anticipated an enemy like this one. He was dead before his mangled body hit the floor.

Responding purely by dint of reflex and being cold-blooded killers themselves, Baker, in front, and Dog, at the back of the house, managed to disenthrall themselves and open fire. But the monster that had seemed so huge only a moment before suddenly became too small to draw a bead on, and it moved with blinding speed. The best they could do was fire on full automatic and empty their magazines.

They came closer to killing each other than shooting … whatever the hell it was.

Still, each of them yelled, "You hit it?"

They both answered angrily, "No, goddamnit."

Charlie ran into the house and with his two comrades looked down at the shredded remains of their late leader. Nobody needed to ask if Able was dead. A moment later, Mateo found the courage to enter the house and see what had happened.

He thought he was going to have to raise the fee the surviving mercenaries would get to continue the job, but he knew this wasn't the time to talk about money. At the moment, these men needed nothing so much as someone to kill. Mateo didn't want it to be him.

As it was, Baker, stepping into the leadership role, relieved Mateo of the necessity to talk business. With Charlie and Dog's unspoken consent, he told Mateo, "The rest of this job is on us. Whatever that thing was, we're going to find it and kill it."

The bear had just broken into a run, charging Freddie Strait Arrow, mouth agape, teeth bared, the picture of an imminent and savage death, when sounds of automatic weapons fire filled the air. The shots didn't sound immediately proximate but were easily heard and held the prospect of drawing nearer and being repeated.

Freddie prayed someone was shooting at the bear, would kill it before —

The beast dug its paws into the ground and skidded to a stop, mere feet away from its intended victim. Animal behavior was not one of Freddie's fields of study, but as he watched the bear swing its head back and forth he thought he saw fear in the ursine eyes. He also saw a trough in the fur on one of the animal's front legs. The exposed skin looked raw and red.

Had the animal been shot, Freddie wondered.

Did it understand the danger of gunfire?

Was that why the fusillade had spooked it so badly?

Freddie renewed his silent supplication for more shooting, but it didn't come. The silence allowed the bear to regain its focus. The animal turned its gaze back to Freddie, looking as if it was deciding which part of him to eat first. While it had the chance.

Possessing the casual agnosticism of a scientist, Freddie nonetheless whimpered, "Oh, Jesus."

The bear took a single step toward him, and then it stopped, raised its head to gaze at something behind Freddie. The bear seemed confused or at least distracted. It wasn't used to confronting a creature larger than itself.

Freddie saw the beast look up and asked himself: What the hell was bigger than a bear?

Whatever it was, the growl it produced made Freddie's hair stand on end and the bear to look for more easily had pickings. It turned away from Freddie and fled, crashing through the underbrush. Leaving its formerly intended prey alone with some new, even more fearsome predator coming up from behind.

That was more than Freddie's mind could cope with; his consciousness began to slip away. A much better way to go, he thought. Unaware of the end as it occurred. A pang of regret accompanied his descent into darkness, though. He could have done so much more if he'd been given the time.

Freddie didn't know how long he'd been blacked out, but as the light returned to his eyes he was surprised that he felt no pain. All his limbs seemed intact and responsive. He could detect no source of bleeding. To the contrary, his head seemed to be resting on someone's lap, soft and comforting. His cheek was being gently stroked.

The blissful comfort was almost enough to lull him back into unconsciousness.

But he wanted to know who was soothing him.

He turned his head to look up and saw Marlene.

She said, "You'll need to get to your feet soon. We have to find Tall Wolf."

CHAPTER 29

Cascade Mountains — Washington State

After patching up Basilio Nuñez the night before with the medical supplies he helped his captors find, John questioned him, testing the man's claim that he could be of help in bringing his superiors to justice.

Basilio, sitting on his camp bed, told John the drug growing operation in the Cascades belonged to Fausto Zara. He also confirmed the new location of the marijuana processing camp that Ernesto had given to John. He told them how many *campesinos* worked as growers and processors: an even hundred. "No, ninety-nine," he said, "after that one ran away."

He pointed a finger at Valeria. Ernesto slapped his hand down.

"Fifteen guards," Ernesto said. "Fourteen, not counting me. Five to keep the workers from running away; ten to chase off intruders."

"Just scare, not kill?" John asked.

"Julián said to kill only if we must."

"Who's Julián?" Rebecca asked.

"That pig's cousin," Valeria said. "He is much smarter, has better manners."

"But he's still in firm control?" John asked.

Ernesto nodded. "He could turn that one loose on us, if he chose." Meaning Basilio. "He told us as much. But if we live within the rules, he prefers things peaceful."

"You think he might feel differently now?" John asked.

Basilio laughed. "Julián wants to be loved by everyone, the *maricón*." Faggot. "But if *his* life or money was threatened, he would kill like anyone else. Like me."

John looked at Ernesto. He seconded Basilio's opinion with a nod.

"What about the other guards?" John asked. "If the workers tried to flee, would the guards shoot them?"

"Some would," Valeria said.

Ernesto nodded. "Some, yes ... but not without this one," he pointed a thumb at Basilio. "Not if he and Julián were removed."

"That or we could bribe them," Valeria said.

"They're all corrupt?" John asked.

"They're all *poor, señor,*" Ernesto said. "The idea of having enough money to start a decent life is a powerful thing."

Basilio laughed and said, "The growers and the guards both, including Ernesto there, they are all *coños.*" Pussies.

Ernesto thrust the butt of his rifle into Basilio's gut, knocking him off the camp bed.

John lifted Basilio to his feet, increasing the volume of the man's moans.

"Always risky to insult a marine," John told him.

Ernesto nodded, sending a clear message more pain was available.

With that in mind, Basilio told his captors that others from the new camp would come by in the morning to reclaim as many things as they could carry. Julián would not worry about Basilio's absence. The fact was, Basilio was sure his cousin would be glad to see the last of him.

"So, if you let me go, I will not return to him. I'll go home to Mexico."

The plea was directed at John. He looked at Ernesto and Valeria.

Ernesto only shook his head.

Valeria said, "Ask him where the bribe money is being kept at the new camp."

John relayed the question to Basilio with a look.

The man refused to say another word.

Ernesto inclined the barrel of his rifle in Basilio's direction.

John said, "It probably wouldn't look good on my résumé if I let you execute him."

Valeria asked, "What if we leave him for the bear? Have you seen the bear?"

Basilio hadn't, but John and Rebecca nodded.

John said, "Interesting idea. If we stake him out and a bear attacks him, that would be pretty much a gesture of fate. Who could be blamed?"

Basilio's jaw dropped. He seemed to think it would be his captors' collective fault.

They staked him to a sturdy tent pole erected on open ground anyway. Ate dinner while he watched. Left food on the outdoor dining table where the scent might attract … who knew what? John laid down the conditions under which Basilio would spend the night.

"Each of the four of us," he gestured to the Batistas, Rebecca and himself, "will take a two-hour shift watching you, in case you look appetizing to any of the wildlife. If something should come along and you need help, just call out where the bribe money is hidden. We'll scare away or kill any predator."

Ernesto chuckled.

"You might need to say please for Ernesto or Valeria to come to your aid," John added.

He took the first watch. Basilio didn't say a word to him.

Just before John was ready to leave, he told Basilio, "If you think my friend Lieutenant Bramley will be the one to feel sorry for you, that would be a mistake."

John told him what Rebecca had done to Serge Marchand. "Left him with just one testicle."

Basilio was greatly disappointed to hear that.

He had been counting on the white woman being his salvation.

John heard a voice behind him ask, "*¿Realmente?*" Really?

He turned to see Ernesto coming to take his shift.

He'd obviously heard what John had said.

"Es verdad," John said. It's true.

"Qué mujer." What a woman. "I think my Valeria might do as much."

Ernesto didn't say a word to Basilio as he stood watch. At Ernesto's insistence, Basilio's shins and thighs, as well as his wrists, had been tied to the pole. He could slouch but he couldn't sit. Whenever the bound man started to fall asleep on his feet, Ernesto would grunt or growl. Basilio's eyes snapped open every time, thinking the bear was coming for him.

Basilio wanted to curse his tormentor, but he was smart enough to know that as bad as things were they could always become worse. He had done worse to others. So he held his tongue. At first, Basilio tried to convey his contempt with hateful looks. The problem with that was he couldn't match Ernesto's glare.

He knew now that in any fairly matched contest, the round-faced bastard would kill him.

Un marino? A marine? Madre de dios. Mother of God.

The bastard had fooled everyone.

So Basilio resisted in the only way he could. He held fast to his secret. He didn't tell Ernesto where the bribe money was hidden. That and prayed silently that if the bear came it would prefer a fat coño to a wiry sicario.

Hitman. Yeah, sure. Basilio didn't feel much like a killer now.

Basilio's slim hope was that he would somehow be able to charm the white woman, who under other circumstances he would have found appealing. So tall and every inch something he'd love to explore. At the very least, the time he spent alone with her would be an opportunity to fantasize, and why not? If a man was nearing his death and knew his last time with a woman was behind him, the next best thing would be to imagine a final conquest.

Even that pale pleasure was denied him, though, when he saw the woman, not alone but with Valeria Batista. The two women had decided to share their guard duty. It wasn't hard to imagine that Valeria had learned of what the other bitch had done to that poor bastard in Canada. Cost him one of his *huevos.*

Eggs. Balls, as the *yanquis* would put it.

Dios, he could see Valeria taking both of his, if he gave her the least excuse. He didn't even look at the women when they took their camping chairs opposite him, each holding an automatic weapon. His whole body ached now from being tied to the pole. His feet and legs felt like they were on fire. He resisted saying so, lest he give the *cabrónes* any ideas.

Still, he listened to the women talk.

You put two of them together you couldn't stop them from doing that.

Valeria asked Rebecca, "Is it *very* cold in your country?"

"In winter, yes. In spring and autumn, about half the time. Summer is wonderful, but it never lasts as long as we'd like."

"There is nowhere warm?"

"Vancouver is mild compared to most other places, but it's not really warm, except in summer. Most everyone who can afford it spends time in the U.S. or the Caribbean during the winter."

Valeria sighed. "*Los ricos* are always comfortable."

Rebecca understood the meaning by context. "Rich people aren't always happy, but they usually stay warm, yeah."

"It is true what Señor Tall Wolf says, you are with the police?"

Rebecca nodded. "Yes, it's part of my family tradition."

"Are you important in your police job?"

Rebecca laughed. "I'll find out how important I am any day now."

She told Valeria the story of her confrontation with Serge Marchand.

Valeria clapped and said, "*Maravillosa.*" Wonderful.

"Yeah, well, we'll see about that. I might have to flee to the U.S."

Just like me, Valeria thought.

"So what's your story?" Rebecca asked.

"I was a *maestra,* a teacher. For the little ones. I was happy. The boy next door, I always thought he wanted to be my *novio.* Sweetheart, yes?"

Rebecca smiled and nodded. "And?"

"I wasn't very nice to him at all. I didn't think he was the least bit *guapo.* Handsome. In school we were always the two best students. He had to work much harder for his grades, though. He was always polite to me, never improper. I was polite to him, never interested. I thought that didn't matter, but the day came when he left to join the military. He knocked on my door, bowed to me and said, 'I will miss you very much.' Nothing else except, '*Hasta la vista.*'"

"Good bye?"

"Yes, but also until we meet again. I never gave him a second thought while he was away. Not until I was twenty-one and I received a wedding proposal from a much older man. He was the mayor of our town. He was also a ..." Valeria searched for the right word.

"A bastard?"

"That, of course, yes. But I want something else."

Rebecca came up with it intuitively. "A front man for some-thing else."

Valeria smiled. "Yes, a front man for a drug cartel."

"Whose cartel?" The question came from Basilio not Rebecca. He'd been listening all along, interested.

"*Cállate,*" Valeria yelled. Shut up.

Basilio opened his mouth to reply, thought better of it and zipped his lip.

"My parents were very worried because the mayor had told them things could go very well for them or very badly. Their lives were in my hands."

"That's awful," Rebecca said.

Valeria said, "I didn't know what to do. I thought I would have to marry this horrible old man, but my parents had another plan.

They went to our neighbors. The parents of my old schoolmate. My parents knew he'd become a marine, something I never took the time to find out. My parents asked his parents if there was some way he might help me. They said possibly."

"They had to check with their son first, before saying yes," Rebecca said.

"That and decide how willing they were to risk their own safety. While everyone was waiting the mayor grew impatient. He was not used to being denied anything he desired. He talked to his cartel friends and they sent a *sicario* — a killer — to knock on my door just as my schoolmate had."

"What did he say?" Rebecca said.

"No one ever found out. Before he could knock a second time he was shot through the head. To make sure the mayor understood the significance of this, he received a note. It was nailed to the door of his house. *Usted y todos los de usted será el siguiente.* You and all yours will be next."

Rebecca asked, "Did the mayor take it to heart?"

"The man who died at my doorstep was a feared murderer. That he could be killed was like the hand of God reaching out to protect us. The mayor hid in his house. What happened next was even more important. A squad of marines appeared at my parents' house. All of them were in uniform and wearing masks to protect their identities. Except for one. My old schoolmate. He was wearing a white tuxedo and his face was exposed."

"That is too cool," Rebecca said, squeezing Valeria's hand.

Tears in her eyes, Valeria nodded. "Ernesto said to me, 'If you would do me the honor, I think you would be safer as my wife.' He and the marines walked me, my parents and his parents to the church. I was wearing jeans and an old blouse. He told me I looked beautiful. The priest was waiting for us."

"What a great guy," Rebecca said.

"There were marine helicopters flying overhead to make sure no one tried to stop the ceremony. After we were married, everyone in the wedding party got on board a helicopter and we left my hometown forever. Ernesto told me he would release me from my wedding vows as soon as he could be sure I was safe. I told him I *never* wanted him to let me go."

Rebecca felt her heart swell. She realized she felt the same way about John. They wouldn't need a small army to accompany them, but it was time for them to exchange a few vows, too.

"Ernesto knew he had to leave Mexico. He had exposed his identity and challenged the cartel directly. They would have to kill him or the other bosses would know they were weak and would come to seize their territory."

"*Sí,*" Basilio said.

Valeria didn't bother to chastise him this time.

"Ernesto crossed the border and came here," she said. "A year later, when he had some money, he sent for me, and now here we are. I only hope we can stay or go to your country. Maybe we could buy warm clothes there."

Rebecca laughed. "I'll certainly stand up for you, if you choose Canada. If my vote of confidence still means anything at the time."

"Your friendship will mean everything." Valeria got to her feet. "*Perdóname.*"

She walked over to Basilio and spoke softly in Spanish, "You heard everything I said?"

He said nothing, only nodded.

"Do you believe I was telling the truth?"

After a moment's hesitation, he inclined his head again.

"Good, because now you know why I love my husband. You also know what kind of man he is. The American man and the lady from Canada are good people, but they haven't known the desperation Ernesto and I know. So you will believe the message Ernesto gave me for you: Tell me where the bribe money is or you will be next."

Basilio told her.

CHAPTER 30

The New Processing Camp, Cascade Mountains
Washington State

Julián decided the time had come to *di-di*. The American soldiers who fought in Vietnam had appropriated the expression from the natives. Julián's father had told him it meant, "Get out of Dodge pronto."

Make a necessary retreat fast.

It had only been on his death bed that Julián's father, Juan, had told his son the truth of who he was, up to a point. "I screwed up my very first semester of college, at a really good school, too, and got my ass booted out the door."

"What did you do?"

"Well, this was way back before the Internet, but I sort of anticipated crowd-sourcing."

His father had to explain the term to him. "It means in any community there's a large body of resources an individual can tap into. These days, the resource is usually money. You tell the group of people 'my kid is sick or has this really great opportunity. He or she needs some money. Will you please help?' You got all that?"

Julián had nodded. He was bright from the start. Like his old man.

"Okay, so I get to college, I sign up for my classes, and right away I think: There are plenty of people here, upperclassmen, who took all the same classes I'm taking. They know all the right answers to all of the tests. The ones who got good grades on term papers know just what the professors are looking for. I saw this wealth of knowledge as a potential resource. So I set up shop in a coffee bar just off campus. Put the word out I was looking for copies of tests and papers that would guarantee straight-A's in the courses four or five hundred other freshmen and I were taking."

"Isn't that cheating?" Julián asked.

His father stroked his cheek. "I looked at it as accelerated learning. I set things up so none of the upperclassmen had to use their real names. I gave each of them a code identity. I charged my fellow freshmen a fee for the information and passed ninety percent along to the pool of money the upperclassmen shared."

That was when Julián asked the question that endeared him to his dying father. "Was your ten percent the most money anyone got?"

"Yeah, it was. There was more money in the pool but it was shared by a lot of people. My cut was mine alone. The problem was, the idea got too popular. People who'd taken classes that would never interest me wanted to get in on the action. People started coming to my dorm room not the coffee bar. It got so popular there was a line out my door anytime I was in my room. People noticed and somebody ratted me out."

"That's when you had to leave college?"

"Yeah, and also when I lost my student draft deferment. Next thing I know, I'm in the army, trained as a rifleman and sent to Vietnam. I can't think of anything but, 'Shit, I'm going to get killed over here.'"

"But you didn't," Julián said.

His father laughed and began to cough. Something he'd done a lot of lately.

"Maybe I did," he said, "that was where I started smoking and now this goddamn lung cancer is going to do me in. Any fucking minute now, it feels like. The only reason I got out of Nam, though, was because the lieutenant who headed up my unit took care of me."

"Why did he do that?"

"He liked me. We looked so much alike everybody thought we had to be brothers. He was real close in age to me, too. He'd gotten into West Point at seventeen. Skipped a couple grades on his way to college. So he was only three years older than me. But he had a world of knowledge I lacked about how to survive in Indian country."

The term puzzled Julián.

"Enemy territory. What the lieutenant knew wasn't something you could buy from another student. You had to go out and learn it yourself. I was starting to feel better about my chances of surviving, learning directly from my commanding officer, but one day he told me he had only two weeks left in-country. He'd be going home. I was sure again that I would die in that damn war."

"But you didn't."

"Might as well have. Three days before the lieutenant was scheduled to leave, we were out on patrol, looking for an NVA company that was supposed to be moving into our area of operation. The lieutenant didn't have to be out in the boonies with us, his time was so short, but he wanted to take care of his men, including me.

"Well, we didn't find the enemy; they found us. The lieutenant was probably the first man killed. He was standing next to me, looking out for me as usual. He took two rounds right in the face. Dead before he knew it, I think. Don't know why I wasn't killed, too, but that didn't happen. I did my damnedest to kill as many of those bastards as I could. Think I might have gotten one, maybe two.

"We called in artillery and air support and the enemy broke off contact. Oh, yeah. All this was happening in the middle of the damn night. Pitch black except for the tracer rounds and grenade explosions lighting things up. It took a while for reinforcements to tend the wounded, recover the dead and get us the hell out of there. I had all the time I needed to do the thing that saved my life, the thing that's haunted me from that day to this.

"I *di-di'ed,* maybe in a way nobody else ever did. The lieutenant had been scheduled to leave the country in three days; I had nine months to go. So I switched uniforms with him and gave myself a good bash with the butt of my M-16. With the bruises on my face and the concussion I'd given myself, I was able to pass for the lieutenant, pleading I couldn't remember anything. The lieutenant's face, all shot to hell, wasn't recognizable; he passed muster wearing my uniform and dog tags. My military IDs.

"So my parents buried him, I guess, and I skipped out of the hospital in California where I was sent to recover. I couldn't let the lieutenant's family see me; they'd know I wasn't him. I could've run to Canada. That's where a lot of draft dodgers went. But I figured I'd rather go somewhere warm, where it would be easier to hide. Somewhere I could bribe people to let me stay, if it came to that. I crossed into Tijuana, met your mother and I've stayed in Mexico ever since."

"But you couldn't hide from yourself," Julián said.

"No," his father admitted. "And I'm pretty sure I'll pay a price real soon. I have a feeling the lieutenant will be waiting for me, and he's not going to be happy."

Julián's father died the next day. Julián never learned his real name.

He was twelve years old at the time.

He made a point of doing his best in school, strictly through his own efforts. When the time came to apply to college, he decided he wanted to see his father's country. He applied to the best schools in California and was accepted by all of them. He was fluent in English, one of the two languages spoken at home and, better yet, he was able to pay the full tuition cost.

Not personally. Neither he nor his mother had that kind of money. They were quite comfortable by the standards of their community but they didn't have tens of thousands of dollars a year to pay to a college. Fausto Zara did. To him, such fees were pocket change.

Julián's father hadn't worked directly in the drug trade. He was a tutor for Zara's nieces and nephews, the *jefe* not having any children of his own, by design. He wouldn't risk having a son or daughter kidnapped and held hostage, used as a wedge against him. He doted on the other young people in his family, and extended his generosity to Julián as well, but if he lost one of them to a rival, well, so be it.

He would avenge them, but not let their fates change his business plans.

Julián felt sure Zara never would suspect one of his beneficiaries would turn on him.

All of the nephews, nieces and their little friends had seen or at least heard of what Zara did to those who betrayed him. Julián certainly had. Even so, he was going to break with his patron, knowing that he would make himself a marked man. His only consolation was that he felt he'd already been targeted.

Mateo Trujillo had called Julián that morning, stirring all his old memories and making him fearful as well. Mateo said that he was in Tesla with his men and would be at the new camp within two hours. He told Julián to have all his workers and guards assembled. The guards were to be disarmed so there would be no accidental gunfire. All of the processed marijuana was to be piled in one place; it would be burned. The final instruction was to pack all the bribe money into travel cases; Mateo would be taking it back to Mexico.

Julián was shocked by the mere fact that Mateo was only a few miles away. As to the rest of the instructions, it was child's play to read between the lines. The *campesinos* and the disarmed guards would be killed. For that matter, so would he. His plan to grow marijuana under the *yanquis'* noses had failed. He must pay the price. All of the marijuana that had been processed would be burned. That, of course, would set the entire forest ablaze. The inferno, conveniently, would also consume the bodies of the people who had been slaughtered.

Time to *di-di,* before Mateo and his killers arrived.

Past time, really. That fool Basilio, going to scrounge for the few thousand dollars he'd left at the old camp had actually, if unintentionally, had better timing in his departure. Of course, he might yet return.

Julián decided he would have to make things as difficult as possible for Mateo. That would provide him with the best chance to escape. It would also salve his conscience that he hadn't simply left scores of hapless peasants to be slaughtered. He summoned Eusebio and Chucho, the captain and second-in-command of the guards.

He told them, "We are all leaving this place."

Eusebio asked, "Back to the old camp?"

"No, go to Seattle or Vancouver in Canada, if you think you can get across the border."

Eusebio frowned, not understanding the boss. "What, just Chucho and me?"

Julián shook his head. "Everybody." He improvised as he went along. "Divide yourselves as evenly as possible, so many *campesinos* with each guard. Set off along different paths. Scatter as much as possible. Go wherever you think best."

Chucho, a practical thinker, asked, "Wherever we go, what will we do when we get there? We'll have no place to live, no jobs, no money."

Julián hadn't thought of that, but he applied his business education to the problem.

He'd pass out what amounted to golden parachutes to his workers.

"You two will have $25,000 each."

The guards' eyes widened with surprise and pleasure.

To them the amount was a king's fortune.

"The other guards will get $15,000 dollars each; the *campesinos* $10,000 each." Feeling inspired as well as magnanimous, Julián added. "Anyone who wants to do so may also take two kilos of marijuana. That amount should be worth another $14,000 at the legal market price. You'll get less on the black market but the amount will still be in the thousands of dollars."

The two guards were all but overwhelmed by the prospect of freedom and so much money.

Julián warned them. "Trying to sell the marijuana could land you in prison. You and all the others have to decide whether the money is worth the risk."

He saw the two guards were willing to take that chance.

"Organize the camp," he told them. "I want everyone on their way within an hour."

With Eusebio and Chucho talking to the fellow guards first, the thought occurred to Julián that all the men with the assault rifles had to do to make far more money would be to shoot him and take everything. They didn't. Most likely, the thought had never entered their minds. It was all they could do not to think that the money — and marijuana — they would be receiving was more than a collective dream.

As it was, the cash Julián parceled out brought tears of gratitude to everyone who received it. He told each person, "You've earned this. Be careful not to let anyone take it from you." They all promised no one would take their money.

He knew only the lucky ones would succeed.

Only a quarter of the *campesinos* accepted the offer of the two kilos of grass.

All of the guards did, and Julián allowed them to take a third kilo.

He told the armed men it was their obligation to see their group of peasants safely out of the forest and mountains. They should do their best to avoid any unfamiliar armed men, but if they had no choice they were to defend their *compañeros*. They all swore to do so.

Julián thought maybe a third would do so.

He was the last one to leave the new camp and the only one to head further uphill. After his exercise in largesse, he had just under $2 million in hundred dollar bills, about forty pounds in weight, to carry in a backpack. He also had an assault rifle, three extra magazines of ammunition and two canteens of water. It was a load to carry uphill.

Not nearly as bad, though, as the 85 pounds his father told him he'd carried in Viet Nam.

He wouldn't have to carry the weight nearly as far as his father described either. He ascended only until he reached a ridge overlooking the new camp. It was shielded from the view of anyone entering the camp below by a thicket of shrubs. Julián had never killed anyone, but he thought maybe he'd kill Mateo Trujillo. Add a line to his résumé, one that would never make it into print. Something he'd just let the guy on the other side of a negotiating table see in his eyes.

This SOB is a stone-killer.

Something like that could give him a real edge.

Not that he'd use it every time.

Not when he went to ask Freddie Strait Arrow for a job anyway.

CHAPTER 31

Approaching the New Camp, Cascade Mountains
Washington State

Basilio Nuñez walked point, lead position, the first man to take hostile fire, through the rising slope of mountain forest, heading back to the new camp he'd left the night before. He had no choice in the matter. Ernesto Batista followed him five paces back carrying his assault rifle at the ready.

Basilio had pleaded with John Tall Wolf to be turned loose once he gave up the location of the bribe money at the new camp. What more could be asked of him? He promised to leave the *yanqui* mountains and return to his homeland.

Valeria had intervened, explained to John, "This man told all the *campesinos* many times, 'I have killed more people than I can remember. If you don't do what you are told, the number will grow larger. Not that I'll remember your deaths for long.'"

John asked Ernesto, "You believe him?"

"He exaggerates the number, probably, but not the fact that he is a killer."

That being the case, John wasn't about to turn Basilio loose on an unsuspecting Washington State public. The confessed killer's hands were bound at his wrists with nylon cord. Ernesto hadn't needed to tell Basilio that he would be shot if he tried to run. It was understood.

Valeria followed ten paces behind her husband, holding the

handgun that had been taken from Basilio. Ernesto had shown her the proper way to hold it and shoot it. Aim for the center mass of her target's body.

John and Rebecca walked drag, the rear guard position. The American and Canadian contingent of the international squad paid attention to the Mexican marine up ahead. They both admired the stealth and sure-footedness with which he moved. How he was able to herd Basilio while also keeping watch for other dangers.

Valeria was less skilled, but it was clear she was trying to emulate her husband's techniques. She made very little noise. Her skill seemed to grow with every step.

John and Rebecca trailed Valeria by ten paces.

At the start of the march, John said both military and police training dictated that he and Rebecca should walk Indian file, one behind the other. What with him being an actual Indian and holding an automatic weapon, he volunteered to take the rear-most position.

The first person to be targeted in an attack from behind.

Rebecca had shaken her head and whispered, "Walk next to me. I want to talk."

John stepped to her right and replied quietly. "If you want to put in a pitch for our new friends up ahead, don't worry. I'll do my best to see they turn out all right."

"I'm sure you will. But that's not what's on my mind."

"No? So what's up?"

"I want to get married, right away. As soon as we get back to civilization."

John took a look around, pirouetted the full 360°. When someone made a statement like Rebecca's, you wanted to make sure no cruel irony was sneaking up on you. Seeing none, he turned back to his true love.

"Okay," John said. "We can hit a wedding chapel in Vegas, if you're in a real hurry. But no faux Elvis officiating, please."

She gave him a gentle elbow and smiled.

"All right, no Elvis. But how about the RCMP Christmas Cheer

Choir singing 'Here Comes the Bride?'"

"If they have the date open, sure."

Rebecca gave him a quick peck on the cheek.

"We're going to have a good time together, aren't we?"

John was tempted to take another look around, but he restrained himself.

"You bet, but *where* are we going to have it? I don't think we've worked that out yet?"

Rebecca exhaled a silent sigh. "If you'll have me, my hope is Uncle Sam will, too."

"I can guarantee that," John said, "but am I hearing you think things will not go well in the matter of Bramley v. Marchand?"

"I think Deputy Commissioner Murphy is going to get the word from on high to hand down a decision that both the force and the general public will consider even handed. Marchand and I are both destined for some post that's cold and lonely."

"Not together," John said.

"Not anywhere close. Canada has a *lot* of backwoods. Thing is, *I* wouldn't consider that fair. Marchand is the one who should be punished, not me. I don't think I could accept that; I'd have to resign."

"And you still don't want me to put in the fix," John said.

"No. So that leaves me with only one choice."

"Marry the Indian and move to Washington?"

"Marry *my* Indian, live wherever we need to."

"You're going to miss home. You'll also get restless until we find something for you to do."

"I know. I hope you won't mind regular visits north of the border."

John smiled. "I remember having some good times up there with you."

"And you'll have more."

For the third time, John felt the two of them were tempting fate, and this time he did take another look around — and saw something. But only when he was facing forward again. Up ahead, he saw Basilio, Ernesto and Valeria had stopped. Ernesto had Basilio proned out on the forest floor to his right and had a foot on the small of his back. He had his rifle shouldered and he was facing forward.

Valeria stood to her husband's left, but she was looking back at John and Rebecca.

She had her teeth bared and held her free hand out as if it was a claw.

They had found the bear.

CHAPTER 32

Cascade Mountains — Washington State

Marlene smelled and heard the group of people approaching before either she or Freddie saw them. She guided Freddie behind the trunk of a large maple and put an index finger to her lips. Silence. Freddie took the gesture as an order not a request.

Like any young male, genius or not, he was tempted to question the assertion of female authority. Unlike most guys, Freddie's mind processed information faster than a high-speed Internet connection, more megabits per second than you could find in South Korea. The first datum to come to mind was that he was alive and well, not being broken down into proteins and carbs by a bear's digestive system.

The second point was that something bigger and badder than the bear had scared the predator off. The fear of the new menace had, hell, made him swoon. That wasn't good for a guy's self-image. That personal failing was immediately rationalized by the reasonable conclusion that no one outside the pages of an graphic novel would have manned up to a grizzly.

Despite that rational assumption, he'd awoken with his head on Marlene's lap. That led Freddie to ask himself two questions: Had Marlene come along after the bear had departed? Or had she *caused* the animal to flee?

The only reason he'd asked himself that question was she just wasn't your average woman. For one thing, he couldn't even guess her age anymore. She seemed to change, not every time he saw her, but every time they went to bed. As if she knew what he wanted at that moment and could sync her appearance to his fantasy. Amazing, thrilling and a bit scary, too.

Frightening in the way she looked last night standing naked at the bedroom window in the moonlight. For just an instant, pushing up through the weight of a deep sleep, he thought he saw her ears had tall points on them. That sent a shiver through him.

When she turned to face him, though, all she looked was better than ever.

God, she was gorgeous. Thoughts of pointy ears receded to the realm of dreams.

Must have been, right? Only just before the bear ran away — *ran away* — he'd heard a roar that sounded like something a Foley artist had cooked up for a dinosaur movie. T-Rex with a toothache. The problem with that idea was he hadn't seen any theropod tracks when he woke up.

Just Marlene comforting him and saying they had to get a move on.

The immediate conclusion Freddie had to draw was there was far more to Marlene than could be observed at a glance. Getting to know who — or what — she really was would take considerable study, even for him. The relevant questions there were: Did he want to do that; did he dare to do that?

Before he could even begin to answer those questions, Marlene tilted her head.

A silent, "Look over there."

Freddie saw people walking through the woods, his forest. A man with an assault rifle warily led a clump of poorly dressed people who looked ill at ease. The group seemed as if it expected to be attacked at any moment. Delivered to some awful fate.

Their desperation touched a chord in Freddie he hadn't known to exist.

He knew the word for the feeling, of course. Empathy.

No one should have to live in such circumstances, he thought.

Certainly not on his property.

Catching both himself and Marlene by surprise, Freddie stepped out from behind the tree, making himself an easy target for the man with the rifle. Guided by some subconscious instinct rather than the process of reasoning, Freddie raised his hands and smiled. Showing he was not only harmless but also friendly.

Behind him he heard the start of another fearsome growl.

If he wasn't just imagining things.

He shook his head and whispered, "It's all right. I'll be okay."

Getting a better look at the group in front of him, he saw the five women and four men were all trembling in fear. Except the guy with the rifle. He was tense but not shaking. To Freddie's eye they all looked Hispanic. He could work with that.

Keeping his hands wide, he bowed and said, "*Bienvenidos. Soy Freddie Strait Arrow.*" Welcome. I'm Freddie Strait Arrow. "*Mi bosque es su bosque.*" My forest is your forest.

The look Freddie saw on all their faces was one of incredulity. Who had his own forest?

The guy with the rifle offered a suggestion. "*¿Es usted un capo de la droga o simplemente loco?*" Are you a drug boss or just plain crazy?

Still smiling, Freddie said, "*Soy un indio rico. ¿Puedo ofrecerles un lugar para refugiarse? Algunos alimentos y bebidas?* I'm a rich Indian. May I offer you a place to take shelter? Some food and drink?"

The frightened people looking at Freddie may well have thought that he was truly crazy, but in their situation they didn't have the luxury of dismissing any charity out of hand. Still, Freddie could see, they were hesitant.

Until Marlene stepped to his side, and all their mouths dropped open.

Freddie turned to look at her and he nearly did the same.

He'd never seen Marlene look better or, to his surprise, kinder. There was an air of a Madonna about her he'd never noticed before. There was an unsuspected tenderness, too, when she took his hand in hers.

"I didn't know you spoke Spanish," she told him.

"I don't speak it so much as butcher it. My adoptive parents were missionaries in Central America for a few years. I picked it up from them."

Marlene addressed the group, *"Hola, amigos."*

She gave them directions to Tesla. Told them there were some bad men with guns in the forest. Hide from them. And when they got to town there was one house to avoid. It needed a lot of cleaning. Otherwise, they were free to lodge where they chose.

Then she told Freddie, "Come on. We still need to find Tall Wolf."

It was the damnedest thing, he thought.

She turned to look at him, as sexy as ever.

But not the least bit gentle anymore.

CHAPTER 33

Tesla — Washington State

R un, hide, watch, report."
That's what Marlene had told Beebs. He'd managed to accomplish the first three of her directives, and photograph the bad guys on his own initiative. But how the hell was he supposed to report?

His only means of communicating with the outside world was to send photos from his Wi-Fi camera. That had worked the first time he'd sent a message to Freddie's cloud, but who knew if … if Freddie and Marlene had gotten out of his house before the shooting started? They might be inside the house that was all shot to hell. They might be dead.

The one area of photography that had no appeal to Beebs was shooting a crime scene.

Especially when the crime was homicide. Involving someone he'd met.

He could, of course, get in his car and drive back to civilization. Stop the first cop he saw and communicate the old-fashioned way, person to person. Only, Freddie and/or Marlene might be wounded not dead. Not dead yet, anyway. If he took the time to drive out of the mountains, though, who knew how long it would take him to find a cop?

With his driving history, all he'd need to do would be speed just a little and a cop would find him immediately and write a ticket. Of course, that was what would happen in *normal* circumstances. This situation was anything but ordinary. He might go an hour without finding a cop. If someone in the house was in need of immediate help, he or she might die in the meantime.

Not that they'd necessarily survive if he made it to them in the next few minutes. He was not exactly versed in first aid. On the other hand, he could load Freddie or Marlene into his car and then get back to the modern world. Welcome any cop who might stop him for speeding.

Sounded like a plan. Only it meant he'd have to put his precious pink backside on the line. That being the case, there was only one thing for him to do. He ran to the bathroom for a quick pee. With an empty bladder, he still might die, but he wouldn't embarrass himself.

Quick as he could, but taking every opportunity to peek outside and look for those assholes with the guns, Beebs pulled his new Civic out of the garage where he'd kept it and eased at idle speed up to Freddie's house. The little car wasn't as silent as an electric vehicle but the engine was soothingly quiet.

Beebs stopped in front of Freddie's house. He could see the shards of glass that had been blown out of the windows. Hell, the front door and the walls had a Swiss cheese motif: holes everywhere. How could anyone inside have survived an assault like that? Beebs' resolve to enter the house ebbed.

He lowered the passenger side windows and listened closely for someone moaning in agony. He told himself he'd go inside if he heard … Christ, what if he actually heard a death rattle? He heard no final gasp, though. Neither that nor anything else.

All he'd done was increase the chance of exposing himself to people who'd shown themselves not to give a shit who they killed.

What kind of fool would he be if he didn't burn rubber out of town then and there?

If a Civic was capable of doing such a thing.

As much as he wanted to, Beebs just couldn't bring himself to cut and run.

"Report," he'd been told.

Yeah, sure, but at what cost?

Any price apparently. Without the least bit of conscious volition, Beebs found himself stepping out of the car and walking toward the perforated front door. No, no, no, his mind told him. But it seemed his nervous system had been hacked and someone else was in control.

Marlene?

Maybe. He kept moving forward.

The best he could do to protect himself was crouch, afford a smaller target to any shooter. That or appear more ridiculous. Make the killers double over with laughter. Give him a second or two to run before they shot him in the back.

At that moment, Beebs felt a wave of fatalism wash over him, displacing his anxiety. He couldn't say he became calm, more like accepting. Whatever would be would be. Just get past the damn present moment one way or another.

The front door wasn't latched and he gave it a push.

Beebs' jaw dropped when he saw a masked man lying on the floor in front of him. Sure, it was a bloody mess. But not exactly in the way he'd expected. The dissonance gave him the measure of detachment he needed not to run for his car shrieking. As far as Beebs could see, and he had a fine eye for detail, the dead man hadn't been shot a single time.

What it looked like to him, something had taken a real good chew out of the guy's throat. It wasn't just a nip to rend flesh. Blood vessels had been severed right and left and a good three inches of the dude's gullet was missing. If the shock hadn't killed him outright, his final moments couldn't have been any fun at all.

Thing was, Beebs didn't feel any sympathy for the prick.

You came to kill other people, look what could happen to you.

For all Beebs knew, though, Freddie and Marlene might be dead, too. He searched the rest of the house, now feeling he'd done the right thing whatever might happen. To him, he meant. What he was doing comforted him, reassured him that he might mature into a man of righteous character. Who the hell would have thought that?

Not him, but he did think of something else. If he found Freddie or Marlene, one of them might have a phone he could use to call the cops. That notion went off the tracks when he saw there was only the one corpse on the premises. On his way out of the house, passing the mangled body again, a new application for his idea occurred to him.

Maybe the dead bastard had a phone on him.

If that thought had presented itself ten minutes earlier, Beebs would have gagged on it. Now ... what the hell? It'd just be going through a stiff's pockets. Nobody to complain. Sure enough, he found an iPhone in a vest pocket, battery charged, with four dots of signal. Tried 1-2-3-4 for the password and found it worked. People. He was good to reach out to the world.

He told the dead man, "Your loss, my gain."

Before making a call, Beebs bowed to an impulse that came out of nowhere, one that had the power to surprise if not shock him. He lifted the dead man's ski mask. Took the guy's picture with his own phone. Saw that he'd been right.

Dude's death had been no fun at all.

CHAPTER 34

Cascade Mountains — Washington State

The humans confronted the bear in force. John, Ernesto, and Valeria had firearms pointed at the animal. Rebecca had her bow out and an arrow knocked. Only Basilio remained unarmed. His wrists were bound and he'd been made to kneel in front of the others, giving him the most terrifying perspective on the predator: a fang's-eye view.

For its part, the beast seem to regard the cluster of people, normally a platter of *hors d'oeuvres* for its kind, with high suspicion. It paced back and forth in a line parallel to the bipeds as if it was trying to figure how the predator had become the prey. Had the bear spied a spot of vulnerability in the line of those who confronted him, he might well have charged.

Only the creature on the ground reeked of fear to the bear. It might have made a passable meal for the carnivore. The bear tried to decide if this one was an offering. Take it, eat it and spare the others. That feeling was highly tempting as the bear was hungry. Still, the others should have shown at least some fear. Had they done so, he would have snatched the crouching creature.

Grabbed it and run off to feast.

Better still, eat it where it was. Make the other creatures flee in terror.

As they should have. That was the natural order. Only the bear's world had been turned inside out. It had been the one to suffer the last time it had tried to find food. Its prey, one of the long-haired creatures standing in front of it, had bellowed in defiance when it charged, and something it couldn't understand had caused it great pain. One of its front legs still throbbed.

Unable to work through its dilemma, the bear continued to pace.

In time, it intuited that the creature seemingly being offered as a sacrifice to it might be a trick. Should it charge and begin to eat, the other creatures might not scatter at all. They might do something to cause it further pain.

The bear stopped its pacing opposite the middle of the pack confronting it. Didn't these puny things know they were defying nature. Such irregularities could not be tolerated. The bear grew angry. It pawed the earth, scattering clods of dirt, and began to growl, the rumble starting deep within its chest, signaling a building pressure that inevitably must be released with a mighty charge to rend the flesh and break the bones of all those who mocked its needs. The bear would sate its hunger for many sleeps to come.

The predator saw the spindly things tense. They were finally coming to understand the way things should be. The way they *must* be. The bear's lead leg, the one that caused its pain, moved forward in what would be the start of its burst.

The second step never came. The bear looked up and, behind the creatures it had intended to devour, saw the monster that had cheated it out of an earlier meal. Once again, the bear felt vulnerable and insignificant, even without hearing the giant thing give its own horrible growl.

The grizzly's charge became an abrupt turn and a headlong retreat.

The animal's lightning change of heart puzzled all the people who'd been ready to kill it.

Except for John. He looked behind him and saw Marlene approaching with Freddie in tow.

"Was Brother Bear about to bother everyone?" she asked.

"Until he saw you without your makeup on," John said.

Meaning the bear saw Coyote in her true form.

Only Marlene got the joke, and she didn't think it was funny.

Julián might have. Looking on from his hiding place on the ridge, he'd witnessed the standoff between the people and the animal. He'd had to cover his mouth with a hand to keep from laughing at Basilio's plight. Served the prick right for running off. He hoped that the bear did take his cousin for its dining pleasure. Shithead tartare.

What riveted Julián as much as Basilio's plight was the unflinching cool of the others. Sure, they had their guns out, but from what he could see even the automatic weapons were small caliber weapons. Hell, you might empty a clip into an animal that size and not bring it down. Even if the bear didn't get all of them, he still might get one or two.

And the woman with the bow, what the hell was she thinking? You put an arrow into a bear that size, you were only going to piss it off. Honey, you weren't going to be nearly so pretty when that bastard tore into you.

Maybe she thought she could put her shot right into one of the beast's eyes. That'd certainly hurt. Might distract him for a while, but if the arrow didn't penetrate the brain, well, the bear would still have one eye left, still have its sense of smell and maybe the archer's scent firmly embedded in memory. The damn thing could hunt her down.

At least that's the way it seemed to an MBA.

He might have felt otherwise if he'd take some life sciences classes.

He wasn't prepared for what he saw next, wouldn't have been even if he'd taken a raft of mythology courses, and he had taken a few as an undergrad. Something enormous appeared among the trees. Damn, it was monstrous. Made him think of Fenris Wolf, the father of all wolves in Norse mythology, the beast destined to kill Odin, the king of the gods.

Julián blinked to clear his eyes, giving him the time to hope he wasn't suffering some kind of mental breakdown. All the blinking did was let him revise his opinion slightly. It wasn't a wolf he saw; it was an epic coyote. Something out of a sagebrush nightmare.

Whatever it was, it sure scared the hell out of the bear.

It turned its stubby tail and beat feet out of there. Julián watched the bear run for a moment. Jesus, it was fast, especially for something that size. Then Julián turned back to … the coyote was gone. In its place was a woman. Looked indio, from some north of the Rio Grande tribe. She also had a face that might appear on the cover of a fashion magazine.

Caramba, what was happening to his head?

He didn't do drugs, not even the kind he grew and sold.

So …

Before Julián could ask himself another question, he saw there was someone standing next to the beautiful woman. A young guy who didn't seem bothered by the shape-shifting qualities of his traveling companion. Then again, maybe he hadn't had the same hallucination Julián had.

Whatever the case, he was the guy Julián had researched, the one he wanted to find: Freddie Strait Arrow.

He'd hoped to have a one-on-one with the man. Not talk to him with a bunch of armed people around. Ernesto and Valeria Batista especially. His prick cousin Basilio, too.

Maybe he should wait. Or trail the group and make his move when he saw Freddie was alone. Yeah, that'd be —

Dangerous. Julián heard something big moving through the trees behind him and a chill raced down his spine. The giant coyote? No, that had to be some kind of mental aberration. Christ, maybe even a mini-stroke. Now, the bear on the other hand, that was entirely real. He was sure of it. That big bastard might have circled around behind him.

Time to introduce himself to Freddie right now, Julián decided.

He looked in the direction of the group of people downslope

from him.

They were moving away. Heading off in the direction of the old camp.

Julián jumped up and cried out, "Hey, wait for me."

In a rush though he was, Julián remembered to grab the backpack with his cash.

He left his assault rifle behind.

CHAPTER 35

Downslope in the Cascades — Washington State

Baker fired a shot before Mateo could stop him. Mateo turned his head and saw a man go down, lifeless before his legs crumpled. A wail rose from a group of men and women near the fallen man. They all sank to their knees and raised their hands above their heads.

A cloud of panicked prayers begging for deliverance in Spanish rose above them.

"Why the hell did you kill that poor bastard?" Mateo demanded of Baker.

Showing no remorse, he replied, "He was carrying a weapon, and he looked my way. I was protecting myself and my men."

Charlie and Dog nodded in approval.

Charlie raised a further point. "Should we waste them all?"

Dog nodded once again, but Charlie waited for Baker's decision.

Mateo looked back at the cowering group and preempted it. "They're peasants. They couldn't describe you to the police if they wanted to, which they don't. Just hold your goddamn fire until I tell you to shoot."

Baker replied, "Somebody's got to pay for Able."

Mateo ground his teeth. "Okay, somebody just did, even if the poor sonofabitch had nothing to do with it. It's also possible we'll run into someone who wants to put up a fight or someone I need to have killed. So wait until then, goddamnit."

Leaving the mercenaries behind, Mateo crossed the opening

in the trees to where the trembling campesinos awaited their fate. Mateo, though, showed no fear of the armed men he left behind him. The three of them looked at each other not saying a word. They didn't need to; they all shared the same thoughts. They also knew Baker was the new alpha.

His look told them: *Wait for my decision.*

They'd need Mateo alive to get the second half of their money, but sometimes there were more important considerations than getting paid.

Mateo stopped just short of the cluster of trembling peasants. He asked a man who dared to glance at him out of the corner of an eye, "Who was that man?" He nodded at the fallen fellow, an assault rifle, sure enough, mere feet from where he lay.

In little more than a whisper, the *campesino* answered, "His name is Gustavo Morales. He was a guard."

"At your camp, where you lived?"

Who else could these forsaken illegals be except Julián Fortuna's people, Mateo thought.

The peasant nodded. "Where we toiled."

"Morales was taking you somewhere? You were his prisoners? Was he going to kill you?"

As a man responsible for many deaths by his own hand, Mateo recognized the irony of his question. Still, he hoped he could find some justification for Baker taking the man's life. But the *campesino* shook his head.

"We were not prisoners. Gustavo was supposed to protect us."

Mateo sighed and reached for another rationalization. "Back home in Mexico, was Morales a soldier?" Soldiers died in the line of duty. That was their occupational hazard.

"No, he was a farmer. We are all farmers or farmer's wives." Taking a deep breath, the man dared to ask, "Are you going to kill us all, señor?"

Under other circumstances, Mateo had done as much.

Now, he was tired of blood, and he would be unable to explain a mass murder to the CIA.

The peasant grew anxious waiting for an answer. He said, "Gustavo has money on him, *señor.*"

Despite the wretched nature of the situation, Mateo had to laugh. Mexicans, with good reason, could believe anyone was susceptible to being bribed. Even the Grim Reaper.

"How much money does he have?" Mateo asked, playing along. Suspecting a pittance would be the amount offered. After all, how much money could a farmer have in his pocket?

"Fifteen thousand dollars," the *campesino* said.

"*What?*" Mateo asked in disbelief.

The peasant nodded and then, as if making a difficult choice, added, "We all have money."

Mateo's incredulity grew. "You *all* have that much money?"

"No, *señor.* Gustavo was a guard. We have only ten thousand."

"Among all of you?"

The man shook his head. "Each."

It took a lot to surprise Mateo Trujillo but this situation did.

Then he came up with a possible explanation.

"Did you and your friends kill Julián Fortuna to get this money?"

"No, *señor. El jefe* gave money to all of us. He called this the golden parachute."

Mateo had to repress another laugh. That business school bastard, Julián, he'd given away a good deal of the money Mateo had intended to steal from him.

"If we give you our money, will you let us live, *señor?*" the *campesino* asked.

Mateo gestured the man to his feet. Told the others to stand up as well. He wasn't going to kill these people. His grandfather had been one of their kind. He wouldn't steal from them either.

"You may live and keep your money. But if you see any more guards with rifles, tell them to lay their weapons down or they may be shot, too."

A chorus of people saying *gracias,* each heartfelt, reached him.

"What should we do with Gustavo, *señor?*" the peasant asked.

"Do you have a shovel to bury him?"

The man shook his head.

"Leave him, then. The animals will clean his bones."

"What should we do with Gustavo's money?"

"Divide it evenly among you. Don't cheat anyone." Mateo leaned in close to the man. "Tell me something, *amigo*. Are Julián Fortuna and Basilio Nuñez still alive?"

Mateo had spoken to Julián on his phone an hour ago, but that was plenty of time to die.

"Julián, *sí*. Basilio left our camp last night. I don't know his fate."

"*Gracias*." Mateo walked back to the Canadian mercenaries.

The peasants were already dividing the dead guard's money, but Mateo was betting Julián and Basilio had kept a large chunk of their bribe money for themselves. He would happily steal their money. Kill them, too.

If he let them live, they would be able to trade their testimony for lenient sentences. Devaluing his worth to the Americans. If he was the only one alive and willing to testify against Fausto Zara, he would be in a much better position.

Unlike Julián Fortuna, Mateo hadn't been to business school.

But he knew all about the law of supply and demand.

CHAPTER 36

Upslope in the Cascades — Washington State

Mateo Trujillo was right about the need to eliminate the competition. Little more than two miles away from where he stood, Julián Fortuna was spilling his guts to John Tall Wolf, who had identified himself as a federal officer. With the Bureau of Indian Affairs, true, but that was good enough for Julián.

"Yes," Julián confessed, "I ran the camp where we grew marijuana."

"Doing this was your idea?" John asked.

"My idea, yes."

"Okay, taking responsibility is good," John said, "but who financed your idea? Who supplied you with your workforce? Who supplied your transportation of people and merchandise? How did you market your product?"

Julián was openly impressed by the tall indio's business acumen. "Have you been to business school, sir?" he asked.

"St. John's for a classical education, but I have considerable on-the-job experience. Now, how about an answer?"

Julián's admiration grew. It was rare to find a liberal arts major with a practical turn of mind. "I can reply only in a general way at the moment. A major drug trafficker. Someone your government would dearly love to place in an American prison."

"You're hoping to gain leniency for your participation in this operation," John said.

"I am the small fish; the other fellow is the whale. It is reasonable, no?"

John sighed. "It is."

"*Cobarde*," Basilio hissed at his cousin with a sneer. Coward.

Basilio was back on his feet, but Ernesto Batista had a firm grip on his collar.

John turned to look at Basilio. "You don't have anything to trade to avoid spending the rest of your life in prison?"

Put that way, Basilio had to reconsider his position. "Yes, of course, I know things."

"But you're not a coward?"

"No."

"Still, you *might* be willing to talk for the right offer?"

Julián, seeing his bargaining position slipping away, interrupted, "That *cabrón* knows nothing. He was only muscle."

Basilio did look like he wanted to punch out his cousin, but didn't deny the charge.

"What kind of muscle?" John asked Julián. "The kind who kept the workers in line?"

Before Julián could reply, John turned to Ernesto and Valeria for an answer.

"Yes," Valeria said succinctly.

"Yes," Ernesto agreed, "but *el jefe* restrained this one." He shook Basilio by his collar. "It would have been worse without him."

Valeria nodded reluctantly.

Trying to rehabilitate his image, Julián added, "I gave all the workers a substantial amount of money …" He paused to choose his words wisely. If he were to say before he released them that would imply they'd been held captive. He couldn't admit that; things would be much worse for him if he did. "As a parting gift," he said.

"How much money?" Basilio demanded.

"Fifteen thousand for the guards, ten thousand for the workers."

"Dollars?" Valeria asked, eyes wide.

"Yes, of course, dollars," Julián said. "I would have given you yours, but you'd left already."

"How much for me?" Basilio asked.

"A hundred thousand."

"Two hundred."

"As you like."

Ernesto interrupted the overt bargaining for bribes. He looked at John and said, "Let's see what he has in his backpack."

John had that in mind, himself. He gestured to Julián to hand it over. After a slight hesitation, he did. John hefted it in one hand.

"All cash?" he asked Julián.

"Yes."

"Mixed denominations?"

"All hundreds."

John nodded, making a calculation. "About twenty pounds here. In hundreds, that'd mean roughly a million dollars." He tossed the backpack to Valeria, who caught it without physical difficulty, but the emotional weight of holding such a fortune proved to be more challenging. She needed both hands to hang on and clasp it to her chest.

"Some of that is mine," Basilio yelled.

Ernesto jerked him back by his collar.

Julián kept a diplomatic silence.

Before the discussion could go any farther, John's satellite phone rang.

He listened for a moment and said, "Yeah, we'll get ready, and we'll watch for your chopper, if it gets here."

He broke the connection and told the others. "Beebs Bandi called the FBI in Seattle and spoke to Special Agent Mulgrew. It seems five armed men arrived in Tesla this morning, charged into Mr. Strait Arrow's house and started shooting." He looked at Marlene. "One of them died badly for his troubles. The others, Beebs suspects, moved into the woods and might be heading our way.

"Mulgrew hopes to send a helicopter with an FBI assault team aboard. They probably don't want the Acting Secretary of the Interior to come to any harm. The problem with that is the weather in Seattle: A storm has moved in, massive rain and strong winds. They can't launch a chopper,"

"Mr. Strait Arrow's welfare would also be a concern," Marlene said.

"Of course," John said. "You know anything about what's happening, Madam Secretary?"

"Mr. Strait Arrow and I left shortly before the bad guys arrived. Mr. Bandi alerted us that they were coming."

"Mulgrew said Beebs asked to tell you he's reported as requested." Marlene smiled and nodded.

"Beebs also said one of the bad guys had his throat ripped out." Everyone cringed except Marlene.

She said, "Must have had it coming."

John let that go and turned to Julián. "You know who these guys are?"

"Mateo Trujillo. He called me earlier. The others must be simple gun thugs, probably obtained locally."

"You might have mentioned that," John told him.

Julián nodded. "I probably should have, as I'm sure Basilio and I are their main targets."

"Mateo will want the money, too," Basilio said, nodding at the backpack.

Valeria clenched it tighter.

John sighed. "The money, of course. You never can forget that."

CHAPTER 37

Descending through the forest

"W here are the rest of the workers?" John asked Julián.
He shrugged. "I gave them the money and wished them godspeed."

Julián liked that turn of phrase. He'd almost said he'd let them go. Again, that would have implied they'd been held captive. He was sure Basilio, the dolt, would come right out and say as much. But, who knew, maybe Basilio might trip and break his neck on their way out of the wilderness.

The damn Batistas could also implicate him in the matter of false imprisonment, but that would be their words against his, and how could they explain their freedom to leave the camp if they had been truly confined? Julián felt comfortable he'd be more than a match for them in an official inquisition.

"Godspeed in any particular direction?" John asked.

"They did not confide their travel plans with me. Only thanked me for my generosity."

John turned to look at Ernesto. "Do you have any idea of where they might have gone?"

While he was still thinking, Valeria said, "Back to the little town. The one on the road where all of us were dropped off."

"Tesla?" Freddie asked.

Up until that point, the young billionaire had been content to watch, listen and sort through this amazing situation. He'd felt safe enough in Marlene's company, even though he had the feeling she'd been responsible for the death of the guy back at his house. Freddie had mixed feelings about that notion. Glad that Marlene had facilitated their getaway, a bit aghast if she'd really ripped out the throat of an armed man.

Having a girlfriend like that meant it'd be a *very* good idea to avoid arguments.

"*Sí*, Tesla," Valeria said.

"I never noticed any migrants in town," Freddie said. "Did you come in trucks?"

Ernesto answered. "We came in buses, dressed as *turistas* not *campesinos*."

Tourists not migrant workers.

John looked at Julián. "Was that your idea?"

He shrugged. "People are more comfortable when you blend in."

Ernesto continued. "The buses had tinted windows. You can see out but not in."

"So they arrived full but left empty," John said. "Pretty damn slick."

Julián did his best not to smile.

Freddie had a question for him: "Where'd you go to school?"

Julián told him and added, "Graduated *summa cum laude*."

"Impressive, but this was the best you could do?" Freddie asked.

With a shrug, Julián said, "No pun intended, but this was supposed to be just my seed money. I have other ideas I'd be happy to talk with you about."

Having her own plans for Freddie, Marlene gave Julián a look that made him take a step back. "If it's cool with your lady friend, of course."

Before a competition started for access to Freddie's fortune, John told Julián, "Go stand on the other side of Ernesto. The former camp boss complied and Ernesto took him by the collar, too.

Then the former Mexican marine told John, "Valeria is right. The *campesinos* will go to the little town and wait for the next bus out. It is all they know."

"All right then," John said. "That's where we'll go, too. We'll join forces in Tesla, set up a defensive perimeter and hope the FBI can get off the ground sooner rather than later."

"How do we avoid the armed men on the way down the mountain, *señor?*" Ernesto asked.

John said, "We'll keep our eyes and ears open. Do our best to be stealthy. Exchange gunfire only if we have to."

Valeria asked, "Do you think we will succeed?"

John said, "Yes, I think so. We have a secret weapon."

With a flick of his eyes he looked at Marlene.

CHAPTER 38

Calgary, Alberta — Canada

Chief Superintendent Edward Bramley, who was both Rebecca Bramley's uncle and her godfather, sat with Deputy Commissioner Eileen Murphy at a corner table in a private room at The Dominion Club, a members only establishment for the elite of business and government in the province. They'd just finished a late lunch, the table had been cleared and, given the occasion, they were allowing themselves a *digestif,* a Talisker single-malt scotch for each of them.

After taking a first sip, Murphy told her friend, Bramley, "The Minister of Public Safety Canada, in his weak-kneed wisdom, has decided to go along with the suggestion of his deputy minister."

"Theo Blanchet," Bramley said, curling his lip. "No doubt after that bag of guts had dined with Jules Marchand."

Murphy nodded. "That is what my spies tell me."

"You have spies, Eileen?" Bramley asked.

She laughed. "Just like you, Ed."

Bramley grinned. "Good intelligence is essential to police work, all right. So you will find Rebecca to be in the right, but she will nonetheless be sent to the rough and remote hinterlands along with that swine Serge Marchand."

The deputy commissioner took another pull at her glass. "Not *with* Marchand but in parallel fashion, yes."

"She doesn't deserve it," Bramley said. "She's a good cop and she was only defending another member of the force and our family, while Marchand threatened a superior officer."

"All true, and you know what? It doesn't matter because both of the pricks making the final decision can empathize at the most basic level with Sergeant Marchand's loss."

"Well, I can't," Bramley said. "Men with balls, in terms of their character, don't bully women."

"I know, Ed. That's why you and I have always been friends. There's more to the story, though, my spies say."

"What's that?"

"While Rebecca and Sergeant Marchand will both suffer in equivalent fashion, soothing both sides of public opinion, Theo Blanchet intends to rehabilitate the sergeant professionally at a much quicker pace."

"Sonofabitch. I won't stand for that, Eileen. My family won't stand for it."

The deputy commissioner held up a hand, stopping Bramley before he said anything she didn't want to hear.

"I'll have my friends watching, Ed. The moment Blanchet starts showing favoritism to the sergeant, I'll land on him like Mount Logan."

Canada's highest mountain, fittingly in the far reaches of the Yukon.

"Embarrass the bastard enough to make him resign? That'd be good." Bramley smiled. "For both of us, I think."

Murphy smiled. "I think we can cast a wide enough net to snag Jules Marchand, too, if that's what you're thinking."

"It's only part of what I mean. If I know you, Eileen, and I think I do, you're looking ahead for yourself as well."

"Well, with Theo Blanchet out of the way and the new Prime Minister in Ottawa, I thought it might be time for me to move to the civilian side of government."

From his seated position, Bramley offered a small bow. "Madam Minister of Public Safety Canada."

Suddenly, Edward Bramley's path to becoming commissioner of the RCMP looked a lot clearer, and his dear god-daughter,

Rebecca, would be well cared for, too.

As if reading his mind, Deputy Commissioner Murphy said to her dining companion, "All this will go much more smoothly if Rebecca doesn't object to her temporary banishment."

"I'll speak with her," Bramley said. "She'll understand."

"Do so without delay, Ed."

"Just as soon as she returns home."

Murphy frowned. "Where is she?"

"My brother told me she went to see her fiancé in Washington."

"That large First Nation fellow?" DC Murphy knew a thing or two about the private lives of all her important people. She made a point of it.

"John Tall Wolf, yes. He's rising quickly through his country's BIA bureaucracy from what I've heard. Even worked a case with James J. McGill recently."

Not much got by Chief Superintendent Bramley either.

He thought dropping the name of the president's husband would impress his friend, but a pensive look settled on her face.

"What is it, Eileen?"

"Just a thought. If Tall Wolf has connections all but inside the Oval Office, he might have more to offer Rebecca than we do."

Bramley's first impulse was to laugh off that idea. Family was family and tradition was tradition, after all. But once Rebecca was married, Tall Wolf would *be* her family.

"I'll sound her out as soon as I see her," Bramley said.

"Please do."

The two of them tossed down their drinks.

CHAPTER 39

Cascade Mountains — Washington State

The trek through mountain forest proved demanding for Mateo Trujillo. He still had the strength and stamina to make the hike, but the temperature was falling and his thin blood, used to the milder weather of Mexico, didn't provide the necessary insulation to keep him from starting to shiver.

The Canadians, Baker, Charlie and Dog, moved with no visible signs of discomfort. For them the weather probably felt balmy. It was all a matter of acclimation, of course. The conditions you knew best always pleased you the most. That simple insight had given Mateo direction for where he would hide once he turned on Fausto Zara.

The weather, for one, would have to be warm. The native tongue, though he spoke four languages, would have to be Spanish. That was his linguistic home, where he could express himself with both precision and feeling. The political structure would have to be relatively stable but the social hierarchy needed to be stratified enough to have a privileged class whose members could buy their way out of trouble.

There were enclaves in the U.S. that were balmy and one could get by using only Spanish. The rich there were certainly privileged, but the justice system sometimes took perverse pleasure in showing the masses that even the wealthy were not beyond its reach. Such uncertainty did not appeal to Mateo. He wanted a new home where the authorities respected the power of a bribe.

He wasn't sure he'd be able to find all the qualities he desired in a new home. So far, he'd been working by process of elimination. Staying in Mexico was definitely out. So was the United States. Those seeking vengeance for Fausto Zara would have too easy a time finding him in either place. The same could be said to varying degrees for the countries of Central America and South America.

Mateo had briefly considered the Philippines. The country had some gorgeous islands. The southernmost of them were where Spanish was most common, but they were also the places where Muslim guerrillas were the most active. Taking hostages and so forth. He didn't need that kind of trouble.

Looking at Europe, there was Spain, of course, but that would also be an obvious place for Zara's avengers to look for him. However, one of Spain's 17 autonomous communities was the Canary Islands. Lying just off the coast of Morocco, the Canaries possessed many of the qualities Mateo was looking for and were probably out of the way enough to be overlooked by his pursuers.

Especially after he left misleading clues pointing to other distant places.

Baker interrupted Mateo's reverie. "Hey, stop daydreaming, we're here."

That they were. They'd arrived at the new camp. Mateo's reverie of a new life had spared him a measure of discomfort from the weather. Which had grown even colder with a chill drizzle just beginning.

Charlie looked up at the sky. "Rain now, snow before long."

Baker smiled, telling Mateo, "A little cold for you, huh?"

Mateo rebutted the man's insolence. "All's quiet? You haven't found any more farmers to shoot?"

He'd told Baker who he had killed, a farmer. Made him feel like the fool he was.

Embarrassed him in front of the other two.

Baker's eyes narrowed in anger. "Wasn't any damn farmer that killed Able."

Mateo couldn't argue with that. None of them could explain the savage attack on the mercenary team's leader. Their best guess was some freakish mutation of a wolf. There were wolves in the mountains, but none of them had ever seen anything with the size, speed and power of the thing that had killed Able.

Still, they all said wolf because if they didn't assert some plausible explanation they'd all have to admit they might meet Able's fate. There'd be no going forward if they did that.

Things were bad enough as it was, having nothing to show for their efforts.

Dog jogged up with an envelope in his hand, after taking a quick look around the new camp. He handed it to Mateo. "Got your name on it. Found it in the one tent that's been set up. Nothing else here worth mentioning."

Baker gave Dog a questioning look. *You read what's inside the envelope?*

Dog shrugged. *Yeah, but I don't read Spanish.*

Mateo did. His face twisted in rage. He crumpled the message, was about to toss it away, changed his mind and stuffed it in his pocket.

"Bad news from home?" Baker asked.

"We're done. We'll head back to Seattle and you can go home."

"After you pay us, we'll go home."

"Yes, of course."

Dog said, "We should bury Able, too."

"Yeah, we'll take care of that," Baker agreed. Still, he couldn't help but think, *If that damn thing, whatever it was, hadn't come back and eaten the rest of him.* "Let's get going."

Charlie, who'd been watching the perimeter, let off a burst of fire. Baker and Dog brought their weapons to the ready and clicked off the safeties. Mateo had his sidearm in hand.

"No problem," Charlie said, waving to the others.

Baker gave him a look. *What the hell did you shoot at?* He hoped it wasn't another farmer.

"Just a bear," Charlie said aloud. "Big fucker. Grizzly. But he ran like hell as soon as I raised my weapon. Didn't have a chance of hitting him. Just wanted to tell him to steer clear."

After what had happened to Able, Baker wasn't going to criticize. "Let's head out," he said.

They'd let *Señor* Greaser walk drag. Maybe the damn bear would pick him off if he fell too far behind. That'd be worth losing the rest of their money.

Mateo had other worries. The note had to be from Julián, even if it was unsigned.

Compañero Trujillo, I can only think things are very bad with Jefe Zara if you have come all the way to my little operation in the yanqui forest. As smart a fellow as you are, you must have made plans to look after your own interests if things went bad for the big boss. You undoubtedly think the few million dollars I have on hand would make you more comfortable wherever you intend to go.

I'm afraid I took all that money, what I didn't already give away to my workers. Maybe I'll also be the first to tell the yanquis everything I know about Fausto Zara. Then they won't need to bother with you so much. Buena suerte.

Good luck.

The smart little shit had figured out exactly what Mateo was going to do.

As the rain increased, Mateo felt he was going to need all the luck he could get.

If he had great good fortune, he was going to ram Julián's note down his throat.

CHAPTER 40

Tesla — Washington State

The *campesinos* were exactly where Ernesto Batista predicted they would be, standing at the side of the road leading out of town, waiting for — hoping and praying — a bus would come by and take them to a city big enough to allow them to blend in with their own kind. *Méjicanos* — Mexicans — preferably, but the poor of any ethnic background would do.

They were a sad lot, shabbily dressed and looking all the more forlorn as the rain soaked them, but for once in their grindingly hard lives they had money in substantial amounts. The plan was that two of the more comely younger women would stand at the forefront of their cluster and wave thick sheaves of money at the bus driver.

This plan would have been foolproof in Mexico, as far as getting the driver to stop. The problem at that point might become: Would the driver give them a ride or try to rob them? In *El Norte* they were uncertain of what difficulties they might face. Were the drivers there paid so well they would laugh at a handfuls of dollars and drive on by? Or would they stop and try to rob the would-be passengers, too?

All but two of the guards had abandoned their rifles behind one of the pretty little houses in town. Several of the women and a few of the men looked at that particular dwelling, so clean and bright with new paint, and their hearts ached with longing. But no one said a word. Homes like that were not meant for such as them. Better to leave your yearning unexpressed.

The two guards who retained their weapons stood at the back of the crowd. If a bus stopped and a fair amount of money was all that was required for passage, the guards would leave the rifles behind. If any thievery was attempted, however, they would defend their *compañeros*. The mere thought of shooting a *yanqui* was enough to make them all ill, but they would not be victimized — ever again, they all said.

As an act of compassion, before standing to the side of the road, they had brought the body of Gustavo Morales out of the forest. It wouldn't have been right to leave him where the animals might consume him. He was the only one of them who would remain behind, buried in the backyard of the beautiful little house where they'd found a shovel in a gardener's shed.

By acclamation, they'd decided to send Gustavo's money to his family in Mexico. They would do so anonymously so as not to draw the attention of *la migra* — immigration — or of anyone else. The gift would seem to Gustavo's family as if it fell from heaven, and when it came time for God to judge them, their honesty and generosity would be a mark in their favor.

They all agreed it was easier to be unselfish when you had some money of your own.

Benevolence was one thing, patience was another.

The rain and their shared anxiety wore on everyone, and still no bus came. Many eyes began to look at the row of houses and shops. So pretty, warm and dry, and as far as they'd dared to look, all of them empty. The idea of spending the fast approaching night indoors was shared by most, if not all, of them and was about to be raised as a topic of debate.

Until a young man walked out of the house at the far end of town. He was not like them. His clothes were too good; his skin was too pale. A *yanqui.* That immediately raised the question: *Were there more like him around?*

The next question, of course, was: *What did he want?*

"*Paz*," he said. Peace. He raised his hands as if offering a blessing. He stopped ten feet away from them. "*Tengo solo un poco de español. Me llama Bruno.*"

I have only a little Spanish. My name is Bruno.

He thought his formal name would sound better than Beebs.

One of the young women holding money stepped forward, extended her cash to him.

Beebs shook his head. "*No quiero dinero.*" I don't want money.

He saw a wave of relief roll across the crowd. "*Habla inglés,* anyone?"

The woman who had offered Beebs her money said, "I do, *un poco.*"

Beebs smiled. "Good." He took a satellite phone out of a pocket, showed it to the crowd. "*Ernesto y Valeria Batista dicen hola.*" Ernesto and Valeria say hello. "*Vengan conmigo, por favor.*" Please come with me.

To get out of the rain, he wanted to say, but his Spanish didn't extend that far.

Beebs turned and walked back toward the house at the far end of town.

He was hoping he'd been taken as friendly, and the two guys with the assault rifles would leave their weapons on the front porch, if they came. The sound of the rain kept him from hearing any footsteps following him. So he jumped a foot in the air when someone took his arm.

His alarm turned to relief when he saw it was the young woman who'd offered him the cash.

He felt even better when she told him, "*Paz, Bruno. Me llama Luciana.*"

CHAPTER 41

Tesla — Washington State

Able's corpse looked even more gruesome than it had several hours earlier, owing to the start of decomposition. Even so, John knelt on one knee just outside the darkened puddle of blood and examined the body. He thought he could see an expression of horror in the dead man's eyes. His last thought must have been a muddle of unarticulated terror. He'd been incapable of understanding just what kind of monster was about to kill him.

The man's fate sent a shiver through John. He didn't care if the others saw it. He was thinking of what his own final moments of life might have been like if his mom and dad hadn't saved him as an infant from Coyote's rending teeth and insatiable hunger.

He looked up. Three of the others, Freddie, Valeria and Julián, looked as if they might vomit. Rebecca maintained a stoical cop face, but a jaw muscle twitched. Ernesto and Basilio looked on impassively, as if their respective roles as a Marine and a killer had shown them equivalent savagery and maybe worse. Marlene, though, was the only one who examined the gory remains with a sense of personal pride, as if inspecting a piece of handiwork that showed no room for improvement.

John stood and said, "We can't leave this body here."

"Wouldn't be good for property values," Marlene added with a straight face.

"I'm going to have this place torn down," Freddie said.

Marlene took his hand. "You could do that, but then you'd no longer have the place where you survived the first attempt on your life."

"The *first?*" Clearly, the thought hadn't occurred to Freddie there might be another.

Marlene released his hand. She sighed. Turned to John.

"Tall Wolf?"

John looked at the young billionaire. "Beebs told us there were four more guys with this one, and they were heavily armed. Given the weather, we'll likely have to deal with them before the FBI arrives. Beyond that, you're stupendously rich and will only get more so from what I've heard. That alone will make you a target."

"*Sí,*" Basilio said, nodding, "*sin duda.*"

Ernesto translated, "Without a doubt." He inclined his head at Basilio. "That one over there, unarmed, with his hands tied and having the full knowledge I would kill him if he attempted to harm anyone here, he is still thinking how he might kidnap you some day."

Freddie, having led a sheltered life and not wanting to believe such a thing could be true, asked Basilio, "Is that right?"

The *sicario,* now deep into his fantasy of illegitimate riches, only nodded.

He looked as if he was measuring Freddie for a car trunk. That or a grave.

Freddie turned to Marlene. "Did you do that?"

He pointed at Able's ravaged body.

John and Marlene exchanged a glance as the others looked on.

Marlene was not going to admit she was Coyote, John knew. Not to so many people. Not to Freddie. He wasn't ready for that. So she had to find the right way to express things. A turn of phrase that would make her rich young man feel safe without being horrified.

She was still looking for how to express herself when Basilio said, "She is the devil, that one."

Marlene only smiled at him in reply, broadly enough for everyone present to see her dagger-like incisors. At that point, it wasn't necessary to say anything. There was no question those teeth could rip out a man's throat. But the glimpse of who Marlene truly was lasted only a heartbeat.

Leaving everyone to question what they really saw.

Was it only their imagination that sent a bolt of cold terror through them?

John was the only one who knew for sure, but now Rebecca had far better reason to believe her fiancé's stories about Coyote.

Turning back to Freddie, Marlene only said, "I *could* kill someone. To save your life, I would do it. I hope you'll take comfort in that."

Freddie did. There was no small measure of seduction in hearing a beautiful woman say she'd kill for you.

John brought the conversation back to Able.

"We need to move this man before his armed friends return. We have to be ready for them and we don't want to trip over him, metaphorically or literally."

Marlene asked, "Are you going to set up our defenses, Tall Wolf?"

John surprised everyone by shaking his head.

"I'll defer to the expert, the man with recent military experience."

He looked squarely at Ernesto Batista, the marine from Mexico.

Ernesto came to attention and voiced his service's motto, *"Todo por la Patria."*

Everything for the Fatherland. And apparently the present company as well.

CHAPTER 42

Woods Above Tesla — Washington State

Sunset wasn't until 6:14 p.m. but with the heavy overcast and steady cold rain, it was dark by five o'clock when Mateo Trujillo and the Canadian mercenaries reached the overlook above the town. Heeding Mateo's suggestion that there might be a sizable amount of money stashed at the original marijuana processing camp, they had stopped and searched the place thoroughly. There was nothing like the chance to pick up some easy money to motivate men to muck through the muddy site and search every enclosed space that might hold paper currency.

They found three one-hundred-dollar bills that had gotten lost in the shuffle.

Enough to hint that there had once been more.

Not nearly enough to reward the amount of effort expended.

Baker, Charlie and Dog were in foul moods when they tromped out of the camp and set off for Tesla. Mateo, at the rear of the line of march, stayed just close enough not to lose sight of Dog. He ordinarily did well enough in rough terrain he already knew, but in this unfamiliar *yanqui* wilderness, finding his way back to the town would have been a matter of pure luck.

He didn't blame the mercenaries for being frustrated when they didn't find the money. He felt the same way. Still, it had occurred to him that a young smartass like Julián Fortuna might have thought it a fine joke to hide the money he'd stolen right under Mateo's nose.

Force Mateo to backtrack after he'd caught up with Julián.

So rather than risk embarrassment, he'd set the Canadians to work for him. If they'd found the money, he would have used it to pay the balance of their fee. There was a risk involved in doing that, though. Having been paid in full, the mercenaries might have felt free to abandon or even kill him.

Now, they wanted to keep him alive at least long enough to get paid.

They undoubtedly could have moved faster than he could keep up. The fact that Dog remained in view told Mateo he was safe for the moment. When he finally caught up with the others on the outlook above town, Mateo sensed that while he might be out of the woods, he was not out of danger. Nor were the others. They all fixed their gazes on the same thing.

The house where Able had died was brightly illuminated.

The mercenaries looked at each other, asking and answering a question silently.

Baker then turned to Mateo. "You turn any lights on in that house?"

Mateo shook his head.

"Neither did we, and Able sure as hell didn't."

Mateo moved closer to the edge for a better look. "All the curtains are drawn, but I don't see any shadows."

Baker said, "Could be a party going on at the front of the house and we wouldn't see it from here."

Charlie added, "With the rain we wouldn't hear it either."

Dog nodded, agreeing with both points.

"I'm thinking it's a trap," Baker said. "Somebody knows we're here."

Mateo directed their attention to another point of interest. "Over there, at the far end of town. The last house."

The thinnest sliver of yellow light escaped from an attic window.

The mercs looked at the narrow band of illumination and then at each other.

Baker told Mateo, "Good catch. Looks like someone thought

he blocked off the entire window, missed by just a little."

Mateo said, "That or it's where the real trap is."

The mercenaries went into another silent exchange of thoughts.

Baker broke the silence, saying, "What really matters is where our SUV is, and can we still use it? Otherwise, it's going to be a long hike home."

"Less so for you than me," Mateo replied. "Canada is closer than Mexico."

Charlie said, "Hey, if somebody else came to town, they didn't walk, did they? Hell, no, this is the U.S.A. They drove. Shit, if we have to, we'll steal their ride."

Dog nodded cheerfully. Baker liked the line of thought, too, but he was disturbed he hadn't been the one to think of it. The world was turning upside down. So he asserted his leadership by saying, "Let's get down there and reconnoiter."

"Rules of engagement?" Dog asked.

"You see someone, you waste him," Baker said.

Charlie and Dog nodded.

Baker gave Mateo a look, as if daring him to object.

He didn't. He only said, "I'll wait here until you're ready for me."

All three mercenaries gave Mateo the same look. He understood their unvoiced insult perfectly. *You miserable piece of chickenshit.*

The mercenaries' disapproval didn't bother Mateo in the least.

He even gave them a reason to approve of his decision.

"If I went into town and I got killed, how would you get the second half of your fee? If one of you dies, I'll still be able to pay the other two, and each of you will get more."

Able might have been up to finding a reply to that.

Baker, Charlie and Dog only departed.

Ernesto's first decisions were to have the camp guards reclaim their assault rifles and then present his credentials to the armed men who formerly had considered him the least capable member of their ranks. He spoke to them in a house in the center of town.

"I am not the man you once thought I was. I was one of our homeland's marines. In the line of duty, I have killed a number of men. The only one I remember clearly was a *sicario* who came to my wife's house to threaten her and her family. I put a round in his left ear and, I'm certain, it exited his right ear.

"I don't wish to waste any ammunition or alert the men who will be coming to this town soon with Fausto Zara's top lieutenant. So if any of you wish to challenge my leadership I will be happy to fight you with a knife. This will not be a game. It will be to the death, and your death will come quickly, I assure you."

Ernesto spoke in a quiet emotionless voice.

John took him seriously. So did everyone else.

There was no challenge to his authority.

"Bueno," Ernesto said. "I will put you in the best positions to both kill our enemies and defend each other. Your first job, and mine, is not to save our own lives but to save the lives of our *compañeros.*"

Julián nodded to himself. Even though he wouldn't be among the armed men, he approved of the message of selflessness. Thought it was good management. He glanced at Freddie Strait Arrow, saw him also nod. Even the tall American *indio* and his woman looked impressed.

The only dissenters were the stunning woman standing next to Freddie, her and Basilio. That fool still refused to believe Ernesto was anything more than the bumbler he'd pretended to be. *Qué idiota.* What an idiot.

"You will not shoot first," Ernesto continued. "I might shoot first. They might shoot first." He nodded at John and Rebecca. "But *you* will not shoot first."

Ernesto looked at Marlene. She shook her head. She would not be using a gun.

"Be glad you will not shoot first," Ernesto said. "You will sleep better if you do not have to shoot at all."

"But if we see a *compañero* is in danger," one of the men asked, "then may we shoot?"

"Yes, good. You see there are exceptions and that is one of them. But all of you put your firing selectors on single shots. You are not trained to shoot on automatic."

John showed his approval of that measure with a nod.

Ernesto told everyone, guards and workers, where they would be positioned and what their responsibilities would be. He embraced each of them and said, "*Compañero.*" They replied in kind. Everyone was surprised when Freddie did the same to Ernesto.

Ernesto, who'd been introduced to the young man who owned the town, bowed to him.

Then he turned to John, asked him and Rebecca for a private moment.

After they stepped into another room, he asked John in a quiet voice, "Is it important that we take any of these men alive?"

"Not at the cost of one of our own," John said, "but if possible, yes. We can learn more from the living."

"*Bueno.*" Ernesto had exactly the same thoughts.

He turned to Rebecca. "Is that a bow you carry, *señorita?*"

"It is."

"Are you proficient with it?"

"I am."

"I would like to give you a place where you may take advantage of your skill then. I will be as far from you as possible as I tend to draw much enemy fire."

Rebecca looked at John for an opinion.

He told her, "I'll be right there with you."

Ernesto nodded, as much in manly approval as professional acquiescence.

"I was sure you would say that, *señor.* In case you haven't heard it many times before —"

"I know," John said. "A guy my size has to keep his head down."

Special ops personnel from Canada's Joint Task Force 2 served with their American counterparts in both Afghanistan and Iraq.

The Canadian troops in Afghanistan were awarded the Presidential Unit Citation by the U.S. government for their actions. In Iraq, JTF2 personnel rescued a British and Canadian Peacemaker Team that was being held hostage. The men in those instances were the *crème de la crème* of their units.

Baker, Charlie and Dog, though deadly without a doubt, were washouts. Worse, they felt the loss of Able's leadership more keenly than ever as they moved into Tesla. Baker took point; Dog walked slack; Charlie in the middle looked for threats on both the right and left. Their search for targets was aided by a momentary slackening of the rain.

They were immediately pleased to see the Lincoln Navigator SUV was right where they left it. All they had to do was … shit, Baker thought. Able had the key fob on him when he'd been killed and then … double shit, that greaser Trujillo had taken the fob.

Charlie crept up close to Baker and whispered, "Damn, look at that. Somebody took all the wheels off our ride."

Baker hadn't noticed until Charlie pointed it out, but he was right. All four wheels had been removed. Not stolen. They rested next to the SUV, and the lug nuts lay right there next to the wheels.

Dog joined them, having seen the situation for himself. "Wiseass prick, whoever he is, left the lug wrench right there with everything else. Letting us know — "

"All we have to do is put the wheels on and we're good to go. Only that prick doesn't know we don't have the key."

Charlie and Dog looked at Baker, dumbfounded. *We don't?*

Baker shook his head.

Well, fuck.

Baker looked both behind them and farther up the road. He didn't see anyone sneaking up from the rear. Didn't mean someone wasn't waiting right around the first bend in the road, though. Up ahead, there was another car parked at the curb, some small buggy about half the size of the SUV. The good thing about it, all its wheels were right where they were supposed to be, and heated vapor from the tailpipe showed the motor was running.

Baker, Charlie and Dog looked at each other, sharing the exact same thought.

Gotta be a trap.

Didn't fucking matter. A working car was still the best way to get out of this damn place and find a way home. If someone was going to open up on them, so be it, they'd just have to shoot faster, straighter and in greater volume. Show the bastards they were messing with the wrong guys.

Charging the car in the same order they'd entered town, the mercenaries' plan lasted all of one stride. Then, without a sound and seemingly by magic, an arrow embedded itself in the back of Dog's left leg, a hair lower than the kneecap. The arrowhead penetrated the fabric of Dog's pants, the soft tissue of his upper gastrocnemius and severed his patellar tendon.

Dog's leg collapsed like the 1929 stock market and his fall was just as abrupt.

Charlie whirled to protect his comrade. With a remarkably accurate instinct he fixed on the point from which the arrow must have come. He even thought he saw who must have been responsible for shooting Dog. He had a target. What he didn't have was time.

An arrow was already coming his way. Traveling at 170 feet per second, it gave Charlie no chance to either evade or block it. Had he not turned around, the shaft might have hit him in a kidney. As it was, the point of penetration was his umbilicus. Thanks to the distance of the shot and Charlie's well-toned abdominal muscles, the arrowhead stopped just short of his spine.

Charlie was in no immediate danger of dying but the impact of the arrow and the sickening wave of pain that followed knocked him on his ass and *hors de combat.* Out of the fight.

Baker hadn't noticed Charlie fall. Seeing Dog go down from an arrow had spooked him. Able gets his throat ripped out by some monster out of a nightmare, and now somebody was going after them with *archery?* He wasn't prepared for this shit.

He sprinted for the small car with the motor running. Wondering what the hell was next. Pots of boiling oil? The mercenary's conjecture was answered in a more familiar and contemporary fashion.

A burst of automatic weapon fire stitched the pavement ten feet in front of him, bringing Baker to an abrupt halt. He pivoted, intending to retreat at speed. Only, looking back, he saw a line of poorly dressed men holding AR-15s. These guys didn't look like trained military, but there were enough of them to shred his ass no matter how badly they shot.

And the guy who laid down the fire to keep him from reaching the small car?

That dude knew exactly what he was doing.

Moving very slowly, Baker gently placed his weapon on the wet pavement. Then he clasped his hands on top of his head. He glanced over his right shoulder and saw a guy with an assault rifle approaching him. He was the one, Baker knew.

The guy who'd fired the burst and organized the trap.

But who the hell had shot Dog with an arrow?

Baker faced forward and saw who. A tall woman with a bow was walking his way. Next to her was an even taller guy, looked like an Indian. He scooped up Dog and Charlie's weapons and handed them off to a couple of the civilians with their own assault rifles.

Damn U.S. Everybody had a fucking gun.

The tall guy stopped a few feet from Baker and said, "Federal officer. You're under arrest. You and your friends."

Trying to brazen things out, Baker said, "What'd we do wrong? Hell, we're the victims here. Someone vandalized our truck."

Rebecca stepped forward and asked, "Where are you from?"

"Ohio," Baker said. He'd never been there but thought it sounded plausible.

Rebecca shook her head. "Bullshit. I know that accent. You're from Alberta."

Baker squinted at her, as if that would help him think better.

"So are you," he said. "I still don't know what my friends and

I did wrong."

John told him. "One of you killed a Mexican migrant named Gustavo Morales. We have several witnesses."

Something in Baker's eyes moved, but not as fast as Rebecca's foot. She kicked Baker's right knee. He fell almost as quickly as Dog had. Ernesto came up behind Baker, reached inside the collar of the mercenary's jacket and pulled out a fighting knife.

"Very good reflexes, *señora*," he told Rebecca. "Very good instincts."

Rebecca glared down at Baker. "I'm RCMP, dummy. If the Americans don't want to execute you or pay for your keep, you'll be spending the rest of your life behind bars back home, I promise you that."

Baker silently cursed himself for having allowed any witnesses to his crime to live.

Then again, it hadn't been his decision, and maybe he had a bargaining chip.

He said to John, "You think I could get some consideration if I gave you a major drug dealer?"

John told him. "Sure, I'll see you get dessert with your last meal."

Baker told him where Mateo Trujillo was waiting anyway. If this prick wouldn't cut him any slack maybe the prosecutor would. At least, he could hope he'd get to do his time back home. Canada didn't have a death penalty.

From the attic window of a nearby house, Beebs called out, "All clear?"

John said, "Yes."

Beebs replied. "Wait until you see the video footage I got. Can you say viral?"

Marlene had watched the encounter on the street from a darkened room on the first floor of the house from which Beebs had shot his video, with Freddie looking on. Everything went as well as she or anyone else could have hoped. In his typical fashion, Tall

Wolf deflected credit from himself. He'd set up others to claim the major shares of praise. The Mexican fellow with the military background had organized the situation with beautiful simplicity. Immobilize one vehicle, incentivize the other, surround your targets with superior force.

Leave the bad guys with only one real chance to flee, and then attack once they made the inevitable choice.

Tall Wolf's woman, Bramley, had carried out her role with brilliant efficiency. Two arrows, two men down. Marlene felt sure her other skills were also top-notch. Knowing that Bramley would spend much of her free time at her future husband's side would have to enter into Marlene's calculations for any plans she made for Tall Wolf.

In a way, though, having Bramley on hand would be a comfort. She would be a defense against random threats facing Tall Wolf. Bramley would help make sure Tall Wolf was alive and well when Marlene came for him in the end.

Tall Wolf had been joking when he said Marlene might not like the way he tasted when she finally got around to eating him. Tall Wolf's real appeal for her, though, was that he made an interesting adversary and a useful tool to help advance her other plans.

She'd never really known anyone else like him.

He'd infuriated her for quite some time, but the passage of time had eased her past that.

The way things would end between them was never in doubt, as she saw it.

So there was no reason to hurry the outcome.

And if she didn't like the way he tasted, she could add a little salt.

From the back of the house, where Julián Fortuna, Basilio Nuñez and the women from the camp had taken shelter, a female voice cried out, "*¡Detiene!*" Stop!

Pounding footsteps and the bang of a door being flung open argued that the command to halt, now being repeated more loudly and shrilly, had been ignored. Marlene smiled. In fact, she was counting on something like this happening.

The time had come for Coyote to go to work.

The FBI arrived while Ernesto Batista was applying field dressings, courtesy of the local, shuttered-for-the-season drug store, to Charlie and Dog, who like Baker had refused to yield their real names. By way of conversation with his *compañeros,* Ernesto had learned that Baker had been the one to shoot and kill Gustavo Morales. While not having pulled a trigger themselves, John suggested that Charlie and Dog might be in line for capital murder charges: causing the death of a person during the commission of a crime.

John mentioned that to Ernesto in the presence of the mercenaries.

By that point, all three mercs had decided that silence was their best bet.

Ernesto whispered to John that first aid might be rendered gently or painfully, if he wanted to get the three prisoners talking. John declined the opportunity of enhanced interrogation. It didn't suit him, and he didn't want Ernesto to complicate his own situation.

So the Mexican Marine applied the dressings briskly but not harshly.

He was working when the FBI arrived in force. Special Agent Mulgrew jumped out of the first of five black Chevy Suburbans. Nineteen of his closest colleagues, all armed and armored to the teeth, kept Mulgrew company, fanning out and looking for trouble. They didn't find any but maintained an attitude of vigilance.

Stepping up to Tall Wolf, eyeing Ernesto still holding an AR-15, the special agent asked, "Everything good here?"

John sighed. "One innocent life lost. Otherwise, pretty good. Those three bozos sitting on the curb are some of the bad guys. The guy on the right pulled the trigger; the other two aided and abetted."

Mulgrew summoned six of his people, two of whom were

female, John was pleased to see, and ordered that Baker, Charlie and Dog be cuffed and put in the cage at the rear of vehicle number five. The federal minions were also instructed to notify the prisoners of their rights.

Once the mercenaries were taken away, Mulgrew asked John, "They're not going to bleed all over my upholstery, are they?"

"No, *señor,*" Ernesto said. "They are bandaged properly and I do not think their wounds are life-threatening."

Mulgrew looked at the Latino guy casually holding an assault rifle. Up to that point, he'd taken his cue from Director Tall Wolf that the man was one of the good guys. Now the special agent wanted to know, "Who are you?"

Ernesto came to attention and replied, "*Sargento Ernesto Batista, Fuerza de Infantería de Marina.*"

"You need any help with that, Special Agent?" John asked.

Mulgrew shook his head. "I worked in San Diego for six years. Nice to meet you, Sergeant. Would you mind handing over your weapon?"

After getting a nod from John, Ernesto complied.

Handing the weapon to a colleague, Mulgrew asked, "So almost everything is good here, after we drove hell bent for leather through a real fine imitation of a typhoon?"

John said, "Before they clammed up, one of those mopes your people took into custody said there's a drug baron hiding in the woods nearby. He's all yours, if you want him."

"Yeah, I suppose I'd better justify the expense of this little joy-ride somehow. But I got word the Acting Secretary of the Interior and a billionaire named Freddie Strait Arrow are on hand. They're all right?"

Before John could respond, a loud female voice filled with anxiety shouted, "*¡Detiene!*"

All three men understood the command to halt.

Only Ernesto recognized Valeria's voice.

He was out front as the forces of law and order converged on the nearby house.

***

Basilio Nuñez used the oldest gag in the book to escape: He had to go potty. Not just pee. He could have managed that with his hands tied in front of him, which they were. No, he said he had to make a little *mierda*. Shit.

That's what he told Valeria.

She didn't like the leering look in his eyes or the smirk on his lips when he told her. "You can watch me while I do my business, *señora*, if you think I'm playing a trick. Also, see what you will be missing by not having the pleasure of my company in your bed."

Valeria spat in Basilio's face.

To her dismay, he only wiped it off and stared at her more offensively than ever.

"Such passion. It is *my* loss not to have you. Still …"

He passed gas, underscoring his need of the moment.

Even so, she was not going to touch him in any way. She ordered Julián to help his cousin.

He laughed and shook his head. "Wipe the shit from that *cabron's* backside? You can shoot me first." Ever the negotiator though, he added, "Put him in the water closet off the kitchen, the little room without a window. I can untie his hands and close the door."

That was just what they did. Along the way, as the women in the house had no guns, Valeria picked up an eight-inch butcher's knife from the kitchen. It had a fine edge, bringing a drop of blood as Valeria tested it with a thumb.

Valeria told Basilio through the door, "You have two minutes, and then I will come in and use this knife on any skin I see exposed."

The *sicario* only laughed at the threat. He'd seen Valeria draw her own blood and it had excited him. "Two minutes," she repeated.

She gave him five. He didn't say a word. He made no sounds of defecation. Valeria began to worry. Ernesto had entrusted her with the job of keeping all the women safe inside the house. That and making sure neither Julián nor Basilio escaped. A verbal threat from Ernesto had been sufficient to make Julián promise to make no escape attempt. Basilio's hands had been bound.

Had been.

Valeria had asked for a gun. Ernesto said for her own protection and that of the other women he could not do that. If the gun was taken from her, things would get very bad. The implicit idea that she would lose rather than use a gun had angered Valeria. She wished she'd had one that very moment. She would shoot right through the door. Hope to kill Basilio where he sat … if that was what he was doing.

She was tempted to run outside and call for Ernesto's help.

Only what if that was when Basilio chose to make his escape?

None of the other women would be able to stop him.

Valeria pounded on the door. "Come out right now or I'll cut off your *verga*."

Literally, stick. Colloquially, dick.

Basilio didn't even laugh at the threat. He said nothing. Made not the slightest sound.

Madre de Dios, Valeria thought. There was no way out of the room except through the door. Even if the turd had managed to flush himself down the toilet she would have heard something. Forcing herself to be strong, at least to the point that her teeth didn't chatter, Valeria shoved the door open and jumped back.

The light in the water closet was out, but the illumination from the kitchen let Valeria see that the toilet was unoccupied. Her mouth fell open in stupefaction. Where could that bastard have … She stepped into the small room.

And Basilio fell on her from where he'd wedged himself against the ceiling.

He wrested the knife from her with one hand and locked his other arm around her throat, cutting off the chance for her to cry out. He whispered to her, his lips against her ear, "Clearly, you don't watch the right movies, *señora*. I will be back someday and we will have a much longer and more intimate conversation."

He ran the back of the hand holding the knife along her thigh, and then he was gone.

Valeria had to swallow hard twice before she could find her

voice.

Then she cried out, "*¡Detiene!*"

Marlene could have stopped Basilio before he got out the back door of the house, but that wasn't her plan. She walked calmly past the women who were taking shelter in the wake of the *sicario's* escape. Most of them probably thought she was going to lock the door through which Basilio had escaped, so he couldn't get back in. Only Julián, in the kitchen, saw the look in her eyes and perceived that she had other intentions. He quickly figured out what they were: She was going hunting.

He told her, "*Buena suerte.*" Good luck.

She replied, "*Ninguno necesario.*" None necessary.

His nod to her prowess struck Marlene as both gallant and subservient.

Two qualities she appreciated in a man. She made a brief mental note to see what became of this young man. Possibly, she might exert some subtle influence over the justice system's handling of the charges brought against him. Leniency might be available should she decide he might be useful to her.

The moment she was out the back door, Marlene raised her nose to the sky. She caught Basilio's scent despite the rain. His fear and excitement hung rank in the air. He might as well have erected neon lights pointing out the direction of his flight. He was headed uphill into the forest. Marlene followed at an easy lope.

The *sicario* thought his best chance to make an escape was to avoid human contact, not let Tall Wolf, his woman or their ragtag militia catch him. Then Marlene noted other nearby scents. The FBI had arrived. Who else would have come in so many overpowered vehicles spewing exhaust? That and the scent of naked ambition to reach the heights of power in Washington.

Well, with her own goals, she couldn't fault others for that.

Once Marlene reached the shelter of the trees, she let her shape shift. Her ears rose to points listening to a chorus of sounds most humans never heard. Her eyes enlarged, processing low levels of light in ways people needed night vision goggles to achieve. Her nose, though, became her most sensitive and wondrous guide. The range and note of scents would have overloaded the human mind. To her, on the other hand, the olfactory sense was the surest path to her prey.

She completed the change, dropping down to four legs, moving at an easy pace.

There were other wild creatures in the woods with her, wolves and a mountain lion. Not far off. The ordinary members of her species would give them wide berth lest they become prey. She, however, was anything but ordinary. She was a creature of legend, and the other lesser beasts knew they were the ones to scurry away from her approach.

Basilio Nuñez was now running for all he was worth, within the limits of his dim senses and thready musculature. Mixed in with his human scents was the tang of metal. A gun? No, there was no sweet stink of lubricant present. Guns were always oiled. Filled with cartridges that reeked of gunpowder. Here there was only metal. The *sicario* had a knife.

The one advantage humans had over wild things was that they could laugh.

She would have done just that in her everyday form. The pitiful man thought a knife was going to help him? Well, he'd learn, and soon. Then she might laugh.

Keeping pace with Basilio didn't require her to do more than trot. Gave her the freedom to search out one specific member of the forest populace ... and there he was. Oh, so hungry, too. From that point, the game was easy.

She picked up speed, proceeded to make as much noise as she could. Let the *sicario* hear her coming up behind him. To his credit, he seemed to have unusually good hearing for his kind. He began to run with desperation. She could hear his breath come harder and even the accelerating, panicked beat of his heart.

The horrible knowledge that he'd become a prey animal filled his mind.

He wasn't ready to turn and fight yet. That would come soon. She ran ahead to her quarry's right and growled. Crossed to his left and yipped. Closed the distance from behind and growled louder. He undoubtedly would have run straight into many a tree if she hadn't been giving him vocal cues as to which way to veer.

In the end, she herded him into a clearing that Basilio sensed would be the arena in which he lived or died. Well, where he could cling to the slim hope that he might somehow get away with his life. That dim flicker of optimism expired when another creature entered the space.

Brother Bear.

Though it was none of her doing, it pleased her to see the clouds above part at just that moment and the moon shone on the clearing like a spotlight. Basilio Nuñez saw the bear clearly, sensed it was the same animal he'd faced before. This time, though, there wasn't a line of people behind him with firearms to drive the creature away or kill it.

This time, all Basilio had to defend himself was a kitchen knife, which might as well have been a sewing needle for all the help it would be to him.

Lacking language in her present form, Coyote nonetheless formed the thought she was sure Brother Bear already had in mind. *Bon appétit.*

She turned and trotted off into the trees. Hadn't gone far before she heard the *sicario's* first, last and well deserved scream of mortality. One fewer kidnapper in the world to threaten Freddie Strait Arrow. To disrupt her plans.

Mateo Trujillo walked into Tesla unarmed with his hands in the air.

His timing was such that Julián Fortuna was just being led to an FBI vehicle for transport back to Seattle where he would be held as the range of charges to be brought against him would be determined by the U.S. Attorney's office. Julián's jaw dropped when he saw Mateo.

He quickly regained his wits and said to John and Special Agent Mulgrew, "That's him, the man who was sent to kill me. He's Fausto Zara's second in command."

His hands still raised, Mateo shrugged. "That's half true."

"Which half?" John asked.

Mulgrew didn't wait for an answer. With a nod of his head, two of his burlier agents grabbed Mateo and cuffed his wrists behind his back. The same way Julián was secured.

Once that formality had been accomplished, Mateo answered John's question. "The fact that I was *Señor* Zara's top aide. I did not come here to kill my young amigo, though. I came to make sure he would be able to testify along with me. Verify what I have to tell the American authorities."

Julián sneered and said, "Bullshit."

Mateo chuckled. "He doesn't know it, but he flatters me."

"How's that?" Mulgrew asked. "Of course, you don't have to say anything."

He recited Mateo's rights, including the one to remain silent.

"That's okay," Mateo said. "I have to talk to let you in on my little secret."

"What's that?" Mulgrew asked.

"For the past ten years, I've worked for your CIA. I'd like you to contact my case officer at the Agency." He gave Mulgrew a number to call.

The FBI special agent looked at John, who, after all, outranked him in the federal bureaucracy.

John took the passed baton without missing a step.

"You know what," he said, "I'll just call the vice president's office at the White House. With something like this, I think we should go straight to the top. Maybe even bring the president into the loop."

Mateo looked at John with disbelief. He saw the tall man's indio features. Could one such as him really have such powerful connections?

Mulgrew knew just what Mateo was thinking.

The FBI man nodded to dispel any doubts the new prisoner might have.

"Director Tall Wolf is wired in right to the top," he said. "Guys, take this CIA-connected gentleman to his ride. We'll hold him until we get word from Washington."

"Just a minute," John said. He asked Mateo, "Did you give the order to shoot Gustavo Morales?"

It took Mateo a moment to make the connection. "The *campesino* in the forest? No, it was the fool who calls himself Baker. He shot before I could stop him."

"But you hired Baker and the others, didn't you?" John asked.

Mateo hesitated a long moment before answering. "Yes."

"Why did you need four armed men to accompany you here?" John asked.

When Mateo hesitated again, Julián answered for him. "He came to kill me and steal the bribe money I had on hand. Maybe take as much of the processed marijuana as he and his men could carry, too." Looking at Mateo, who was glaring at him hatefully now, Julián made a spot-on guess. "If he truly is betraying Fausto Zara, he was looking to pad his retirement fund."

Mulgrew asked Mateo, "Any rebuttal?"

"I want to speak with my CIA case officer. That is all I have to say."

"Sure, but as Director Tall Wolf said, we'll see what the White House says first."

Mateo and Julián were led off to separate SUVs.

Mulgrew shook John's hand. "Nicely done, Mr. Director. I don't know how all this is going to play out, but better it should happen in DC than Seattle."

John said, "Yeah, well, that's why we get the big money."

Beebs screened the video of the takedown of the mercenaries shortly after the FBI left town. His audience consisted of John,

Rebecca, Freddie, Marlene, Ernesto and Valeria. He told John, "I didn't want to take a chance on the feds grabbing it. You know, except for you. You're cool."

"Thanks," John said. He gestured to Marlene. "But you're forgetting the Acting Secretary of the Interior."

Beebs looked at her and blinked. "Is that who you are?"

She nodded.

"Sorry," Beebs said. "No offense intended."

Marlene only grinned, in a way that still sent a chill through Beebs.

The photographer quickly moved on to show the video on his iBook laptop. The capture of the three mercenaries looked easy as pie. Well planned and executed. Everyone complimented Rebecca on her archery. Ernesto said, "¡Viva Canada!"

Marlene asked Rebecca, "If it had been necessary, could you have made your shots fatal hits?"

With a straight face, she replied, "If necessary, yes."

John asked Beebs, "Just in case I wasn't such a good guy, you sent copies of the video to a couple of cloud servers, right?"

After a moment's hesitation, Beebs nodded.

"Good," John said. "Keep their locations to yourself, but in the meantime, I'd appreciate it if you sent a copy to my phone and another to a friend at the FBI. He's a good guy, and I think he should see this."

John gave Beebs his phone number and one for FBI Deputy Director Byron DeWitt.

With that business concluded, Ernesto Batista cleared his throat and asked John, "What will happen to my wife and me? Us and our countrymen."

John thought about that for a moment. "Immigration issues really aren't my responsibility. You want to pick up the ball, Madam Acting Secretary?"

Marlene shook her head. She thought the arrival of Europeans in the 15th century was the immigration problem to worry about. Those people showed no sign of going home.

John continued, "As I see things, most people who were born here are concerned about losing jobs and their local culture to newcomers. It'd be a good idea for everyone to learn English. That way, if someone's bad-mouthing you, you can return the favor in a language they'll understand. In terms of jobs, if someone were to create them for you and your friends, the competitive pressure for existing job openings would not increase."

John looked at Freddie, who grinned back at him.

"I've already been thinking about that. Having skilled farmers and arable land available, developing artisanal crops might be a cool business to get into."

Ernesto frowned. "Marijuana?"

"No, no. People should be able to get high on good food and the company of good friends."

"And music," Valeria said.

"And visual art," Beebs added.

"All that," John agreed. Looking at Marlene, he added, "The telling of tall tales, too."

Freddie quickly outlined a management and labor proposal to Ernesto: A living wage, profit sharing, health coverage, education assistance and, best of all, the freedom to say *adios* if you wanted to move on.

Freddie's law firm would also represent the workers on immigration issues.

Initially, the new workers could stay in the vacant houses in town.

Other plans would be developed as the business warranted.

With the general situation well in hand, John asked Freddie for a personal favor.

"I'd like to borrow your plane."

"Going back to D.C.?"

"With a stop here and there along the way. Might need it for a week or so."

"Take it. I kind of like the bigger plane I chartered to get out here. Using that for a while would be smart before I decide if I want to buy one."

A billionaire who analyzed things before he threw his money around, John thought. The kid just might wind up owning a nice chunk of the country. John patted Freddie on the shoulder and said thanks.

John's last conversation before leaving was a private one with Marlene.

"I heard you stepped out for a short while after Basilio Nuñez made his getaway."

"If you heard it, it must be true."

"I didn't want to say anything in front of anyone else, but I assume the guy won't bother Freddie or anyone else ever again."

"No, he won't."

"Fine by me," John told her. He stared into Marlene's predatory eyes and saw a hint of what had happened to the *sicario*. He looked her up and down in a way that actually made her feel uncomfortable.

"What are you doing, Tall Wolf? Leering is unlike you."

"I'm not leering. I'm looking and I just can't see it."

"See what?"

"If you ate that guy, there'd have to be a sign on you somewhere. A little bulge in your tummy or something."

"I didn't eat him," Marlene snapped.

"If you didn't, something did. I saw it in your eyes."

The idea that John could read her mind scared Marlene.

"The *bear*," John said with a smile. "You fed the killer to the bear. That's a good one."

Marlene was at a loss how Tall Wolf could understand her so completely.

John gave her a wink and said, "Go easy on Freddie. The kid has great potential."

Driving back to Seattle, Rebecca asked John, "What were you and your boss talking about?"

"Marlene? I asked if she wanted to come to our wedding. She

begged off."

Rebecca knew he was BS-ing her, but she decided to let the matter ride.

"So who are we going to invite to our spur-of-the-moment ceremony?"

John said, "Your parents and mine. If you don't mind, I'd like to have Byron DeWitt be my best man, if he can make it. Is there anyone you'd like for a maid of honor?"

"Maybe Celine Dion, if she's in town."

"You're joking, but with my connections …"

"Don't you dare. Our parents and your friend will be fine."

"Something's bothering you," John said. "Your career situation?"

She nodded. "Those hosers we caught back in Tesla? They're Canadian."

"Uh-huh."

"And that Beebs kid did a real nice job of shooting his video. And if I have to say so, I did a pretty nice job with that bow. So how long do you think it will be before the whole world, including Canada, sees what we did? And by we I mean me."

John said, "Probably not long at all, but so what? You're a heroine, if that word is still politically correct. You've got no worries there."

"I've been telling myself that, but I'm still not convinced. I think it's going to have some kind of unexpected impact."

John said, "I'm the last one to doubt anyone's intuition, but you know whatever happens we'll see it through together, right?"

"I do know that, and if you can't fix it, I'll ask your mom to cast a spell on someone."

Serafina Wolf y Padilla being a witch among other things.

John laughed. "She'd do it for you, too."

CHAPTER 44

Monday October 19, 2015, Las Vegas, Nevada

Clark County required no waiting period to receive a marriage license. You filled out a form, showed a legal ID and paid a fee. *Voila.* You were good to go. There was also no requirement that the ceremony take place in a hokey, commercial wedding chapel.

John was a nominal Catholic. Rebecca was a Christmas and Easter Protestant. They found a Unitarian minister willing to marry them in his home. The man and his wife were transplants from Boston. The home they'd had built for themselves was the only Cape Cod in their subdivision. The nuptials were to take place in their parlor.

Freddie Strait Arrow's Gulfstream had to take on a relief crew to fly first to Calgary and pick up Rebecca's parents, Inspector Peter Bramley and Ms. Reva Bramley. Washington, DC was the next stop, where FBI Deputy Director Byron DeWitt came aboard. Dr. Haden Wolf and Ms. Serafina Wolf y Padilla joined the wedding guests in Albuquerque, New Mexico. From there it was just a quick hop to Las Vegas.

While the guests were still in the air, the bride and groom went shopping for their wedding outfits. Rebecca chose a high-necked, long-sleeved french vanilla mini-dress by St. Laurent that showed a yard of gorgeous legs. In her heels, Rebecca stood within an inch of her groom's height. John went with a Hugo Boss classic fit wool suit in navy blue.

The guests also dressed to the nines. After hugs, handshakes and busses to the parents and in-laws, John asked for a moment alone with Byron DeWitt. The deputy director handed John a pair of house-keys and his cell phone.

"Your honeymoon digs on the beach in Santa Barbara. The ocean's in plain view, the amenities include everything you could ask for and the weather is perfect. But then it usually is."

"No earthquakes on the calendar?" John asked.

"Only the ones you and your lovely bride provide."

John supposed he'd asked for that one. He asked DeWitt, "You spoke with Mr. McGill?"

The deputy director nodded. "All you have to do is hit number 1 on the phone. His office is on speed dial. He's expecting your call."

"You shared the video with him?"

"I did. The vice president and the president also saw it. Everybody was quite impressed with the future Mrs. Tall Wolf's archery. Go ahead, make the call. Oh, one more thing. The vice president really wanted to come with me, but she didn't want all her security people to be a bother for you."

"That was very kind of her. I'll have to send her my thanks."

"Your getting married also made her want to push up our wedding date," DeWitt said.

John asked, "Are you ready?"

"I am. Mr. McGill's been giving me pointers. Go on, make the call. You don't want to keep your bride waiting. I'll stall them for a minute or two."

DeWitt strolled off to keep his promise and John hit 1.

James J. McGill answered on the first ring. "Director Tall Wolf?"

"Yes, sir."

"I saw the video Deputy Director DeWitt sent me. I also took the liberty of reviewing Lieutenant Bramley's service record with the RCMP. That's quite the impressive woman you're marrying."

"She is. I believe you'd know something about that."

McGill laughed. "I do, without a doubt. Regarding the idea you've raised, I think it's a real possibility, but I would want to talk with Ms. Bramley. Or should I say Mrs. Tall Wolf? Has she made up her mind about how she'd like to be addressed?"

John said, "We've discussed it. She said whatever works to her advantage for the occasion at hand."

McGill laughed. "I like that. Well, the two of you talk about the idea, and I'll be happy to speak with her."

"Thank you, sir."

"My best wishes to both of you, and the president also sends her regards."

John rejoined the others and returned DeWitt's phone to him.

His mother gave him a nudge. "You don't need your sunglasses right now, do you?"

John took off his Ray-Bans and turned to look at his bride.

"Business call?" Rebecca asked.

John said, "Made sure our table at Denny's is ready when we leave here."

DeWitt grinned and asked Rebecca, "You do know what you're getting into, right?"

Before she could reply, Reverend Dexter asked, "Is everyone ready?"

They were. The Bramleys stood next to John; the Wolfs stood next to Rebecca. DeWitt stood behind John's right shoulder. To keep him from making a break for the door, he'd later joke.

Dexter said, "We are here today in the company of family and a friend and in the sight of God to join Rebecca and John in wedlock. Love consists of this, that two people protect and touch and greet one another. What greater thing is there for two human souls than to feel that they are joined together ..."

CHAPTER 45

Tuesday, October 20, 2015, Santa Barbara, California

John and Rebecca walked hand in hand along Butterfly Beach just as the sun was cresting the eastern horizon. They had the place to themselves. Rebecca kicked at the white foam of the small waves as they rolled onto the beach and receded out into the deep.

Wearing a look of mock insecurity, John asked, "Our wedding night wasn't that disappointing, was it?"

She gave him an elbow to the ribs, a gentle one.

"No, not disappointing at all. I figure you've got about five good years left in you."

John laughed. "I hope so, and maybe a few more."

Rebecca said, "It's just ... I took a look at the *Toronto Sun* online before you woke up."

"And?" John asked.

"Home page, top story. Yours truly in her dress uniform. Annie Oakley with arrows or something like that. Ottawa is very embarrassed about the bad guys being Canadian but couldn't be more pleased about me."

"That'll make you a lot harder to banish to the hinterlands," John said.

"Maybe. I still think there's a boom about to be lowered."

John put an arm around his new wife's shoulders. "I know we said we wouldn't get each other any wedding gifts until we both had time to do it, but I couldn't wait."

Rebecca looked up at John, something she had to do when they were barefoot.

"What did you do?"

"I didn't try to pressure your government."

"Good."

"I did try to provide you with an alternative or two."

"Like what?"

"Have you heard that James J. McGill's investigations agency is expanding. Besides the one in DC there's another in Paris."

"You want us to move to France?"

John shook his head. "What Byron tells me, there are going to be offices opening in Chicago and Los Angeles, too."

"You want to move to one of those cities?"

"Not necessarily. I spoke with Mr. McGill just before the ceremony got started yesterday and talked to him about the possibility of opening an office in Toronto with you as the person running it."

Rebecca stopped dead in her tracks. "What did he say?"

"He said he'd think about it and he's willing to discuss the idea with you."

"He saw the video, didn't he?"

John nodded. "On his own initiative, he also got a look at your service record."

"He can do that?" Rebecca asked, surprised.

"Apparently. One other thing, if Toronto doesn't work out for whatever reason, Byron is going to be the head of the L.A. office. He said you'd be welcome there, but you'd have to settle for being number two in the office."

Rebecca resumed walking. "I'd also have to learn a new city, a new country, new laws."

"The winters are milder than in Canada, I hear."

"There is that." Rebecca said with a laugh. She looked around. "This is a gorgeous place."

"What about us? Do you want to go to work for Mr. McGill, too?"

"No, not yet anyway. I like what I'm doing, and someone has to keep an eye on Marlene. But with you in the private sector, you'll have more freedom to set your own schedule. We should have more time together, and I promise not to marry anyone else while you're not looking."

"Sure, I've just shown you how dangerous I can be. But if we want to have kids, and I do, what then?"

"We'll adjust accordingly. I like my job, but I'm not wed to it. Just you."

"Good. As pretty and warm as it is here, I think I'd choose Toronto first, if I have the choice."

"If you don't stay in the RCMP and make all of my scheming irrelevant."

"Do you have your phone on you?"

John nodded. He dug it out of a pocket and handed it to her.

"Calling home?"

"Calling Deputy Commissioner Murphy. I want this sorted out right now."

"How much time you think you'll need?"

"Ten minutes will probably do it."

"I'll give you thirty. I'll go get us a couple of nutritionally balanced but refreshing drinks."

"Don't forget the straws," Rebecca said.

She watched John jog off on the hard-packed, wave-washed sand, thought about gaining a husband and maybe losing her country. She sat facing the ocean and made the call. Deputy Commissioner Murphy answered by saying, "I've never had a call from the American Bureau of Indian Affairs before. To whom do I have the pleasure of speaking? Is this Lieutenant Bramley's sweet-heart?"

Rebecca laughed. "No, Eileen, it's me, and I'm speaking to you informally because I'd like this to be a woman-to-woman conversation."

"Sure. You want to know where things stand, if I'm not mistaken."

"You're not."

The deputy commissioner told Rebecca about the behind the scenes scheming by the Marchands and the counter-plotting by the Bramleys and herself.

"We thought we had things all worked out, and then you had to go all *Hunger Games* on us."

"So where does that leave me?" Rebecca asked.

"Well, there's no way anyone in the government is going to exile you now. That's the good news. The regrettable news is that your fate and Serge Marchand's are still tied together. If you can't be banished, neither can he. He'll be reassigned in an equivalent post in another province, probably Quebec."

"He's the one who should be punished," Rebecca said.

Murphy sighed. "The prevailing opinion among most of our male counterparts is that you've punished him quite enough."

"Shit."

"Yes, indeed. So can you live with what I've told you?"

Rebecca didn't need a heartbeat to think about it. "No."

"No?"

Rebecca told the deputy commissioner that she had married her American, and she had one and maybe two job offers in the private sector.

"Here or there?" Murphy asked.

"One in each country."

"You're sure you want to leave the force and possibly your country?"

"If Marchand stays, yes. If I go, you'll see to it that he doesn't get to stay."

A laugh came from the deputy commissioner. "Oh, yes, I'll see to it. I don't care who tries to fight me on that."

"Thank you, Eileen."

"Send me a post card if you stay down south, Rebecca, and make sure you have a room for me if I want to go somewhere warm in the winter. I'll tell you all about Serge Marchand's final days on the force."

"I can't wait," Rebecca said.

She broke the connection, and looked out at the ocean rolling onto the California beach.

Maybe the place she'd learn to call home.

As the sun continued its climb, she grew warm and thirsty.

She felt she could use something nutritionally balanced and refreshing.

Looking to her left she saw John approaching with a cup in each hand.

ABOUT THE AUTHOR

Joseph Flynn has been published both traditionally — Signet Books, Bantam Books and Variance Publishing — and through his own imprint, Stray Dog Press, Inc. Both major media reviews and reader reviews have praised his work. Booklist said, "Flynn is an excellent storyteller." The Chicago Tribune said, "Flynn [is] a master of high-octane plotting." The most repeated reader comment is: Write faster, we want more.

Contact Joe at Hey Joe on his website: *www.josephflynn.com*. You can also read excerpts of all of Joe's books on his website. All of Joseph Flynn's novels may be purchased online.

The Jim McGill Series
The President's Henchman, A Jim McGill Novel [#1]
The Hangman's Companion, A JimMcGill Novel [#2]
The K Street Killer, A JimMcGill Novel [#3]
The Last Ballot Cast: Part 1, A JimMcGill Novel [#4]
The Last Ballot Cast: Part 2, A JimMcGill Novel [#5]
The Devil on the Doorstep, A Jim McGill Novel [#6]
The Good Guy with a Gun, A Jim McGill Novel [#7]
The Echo of the Whip, A Jim McGill Novel [#8]
The Daddy's Girl Decoy, A Jim McGill Novel [#9]
The Last Chopper Out, A Jim McGill Novel [#10]
The King of Mirth, A Jim McGill Novel [#11]

McGill's Short Cases 1-3

The Ron Ketchum Mystery Series
Nailed, A Ron Ketchum Mystery [#1]
Defiled, A Ron Ketchum Mystery [#2]
Impaled, A Ron Ketchum Mystery [#3]

The John Tall Wolf Series
Tall Man in Ray-Bans, A John Tall Wolf Novel [#1]
War Party, A John Tall Wolf Novel [#2]
Super Chief, A John Tall Wolf Novel [#3]
Smoke Signals, A John Tall Wolf Novel [#4]
Big Medicine, A John Tall Wolf Novel [#5]
Powwow in Paris, A John Tall Wolf Novel [#6]

The Zeke Edison Series
Kill Me Twice, A Zeke Edison Novel [#1]

Stand Alone Novels
The Concrete Inquisition
Digger
The Next President
Hot Type
Farewell Performance
Gasoline, Texas
Round Robin, A Love Story of Epic Proportions
One False Step
Blood Street Punx
Still Coming
Still Coming Expanded Edition
Hangman — A Western Novella
Pointy Teeth, Twelve Bite-Size Stories

www.ingramcontent.com/pod-product-compliance
Lightning Source LLC
Chambersburg PA
CBHW060917180626
46817CB00004B/1298